THE BLACKSTONE WOLF

ALSO BY ALICIA MONTGOMERY

THE TRUE MATES SERIES

Fated Mates

Blood Moon

Romancing the Alpha

Witch's Mate

Taming the Beast

Tempted by the Wolf

THE LONE WOLF DEFENDERS SERIES

Killian's Secret

Loving Quinn

All for Connor

THE BLACKSTONE MOUNTAIN SERIES

The Blackstone Dragon Heir

The Blackstone Bad Dragon

The Blackstone Bear

ABOUT THE AUTHOR

Alicia Montgomery has always dreamed of becoming a romance novel writer. She started writing down her stories in now long-forgotten diaries and notebooks, never thinking that her dream would come true. After taking the well-worn path to a stable career, she is now plunging into the world of self-publishing.

f facebook.com/aliciamontgomeryauthor

 twitter.com/amontromance

BB bookbub.com/authors/alicia-montgomery

THE BLACKSTONE WOLF

BLACKSTONE MOUNTAIN BOOK 4

ALICIA MONTGOMERY

CHAPTER ONE

THE DEN WAS HOPPING, even for a weekday night. It was, after all, the most well-known after-hours shifter haunt in town.

Same shit, different night, Nathan Caldwell thought to himself as he took a sip from his beer. His wolf growled in agreement, feeling just as restless as him.

"Yo, Nathan! All by yourself again?"

Nathan whipped his head around toward the sound of the voice. "Well, Rogers, unlike you, I don't need a whole entourage to scope out a bar. Did you bring your make-up artist and hairdresser?"

Daniel Rogers laughed, then clasped the hand Nathan offered. "Good to see you, man."

"Just because I like to look good doesn't mean I'm a pansy," Gabriel Russel said. He ran a hand through his long blonde locks and gave his head an exaggerated toss, then flashed a megawatt smile to no one in particular. There was a reason the Rangers called him "Pretty Boy."

"You boys finally got a night off?" Nathan asked.

"Yeah, well, we're taking double shifts," Anders Stevens, the dark-haired man on Daniel's right said. "The boss is having a hard time filling positions. We've put ads out all over the country and everything."

Nathan could guess why. Though working as a Blackstone Mountain Ranger was a lucrative position (it was especially difficult for their kind to get ahead), it involved long hours and living deep in the mountains.

Most shifters were social creatures, and many who lived in Blackstone preferred to work in the mines or in town. Nathan himself was Chief Engineer at the Blackstone Mines, and except for a couple days a month, the hours were easy and left him lots of time to pursue other things. Mostly that involved hanging out at The Den and chasing pussy. Or at least it used to until a few months ago, when his friends starting pairing off with their mates.

First it was Matthew, then Jason, and now Ben. It wasn't that he wasn't happy for them or that he didn't like their mates. Catherine, Christina, and Penny were all great people. But who wanted to be stuck with just one person for the rest of their lives?

Gabriel waved a hand in front of him. "Bro, you okay?"

"Huh?" Nathan's thoughts snapped back to the present. "Yeah, just ... you know, scouting around."

"Gotcha," Gabriel said with a wink. "See anyone interesting?"

Nathan quickly scanned the bar and saw a group of four girls at one of the tables in the middle. They weren't over-dressed or self-conscious, so they weren't out-of-towners coming for a look-see at the shifters. And of course, his own wolf could tell they were definitely not human.

"Well, boys, what do you think?" Gabriel asked. "Looks like there's enough to go around."

One of the women turned their way, a pretty, petite blonde. She locked eyes with Nathan and then flashed him a flirtatious smile and a slight nod.

Anders chuckled. "Now that's definitely an invitation."

"I'm game if you guys are," Daniel said, and Anders nodded in agreement.

His wolf whined in protest. It had been doing that for a while now, like it was no longer interested in the thrill of the chase. *Maybe I'm just tired from work*, Nathan thought but supposed he did have a reputation to maintain. "After you." They all grabbed their drinks and walked to the table.

"Hello, ladies," Gabriel began. "Mind if we join you?"

Before they could say anything, Anders piped in. "We've been stuck up in the mountains for a couple days now. My friends and I are part of the Blackstone Rangers."

"You guys are Rangers?" one of them, a cute brunette said. "You must see some pretty nice sights up there."

"Not as pretty as you," Daniel added with a wink which made the girl giggle.

Nathan rolled his eyes mentally, but the girls seemed to lap it up and made space for them. The three Rangers, being good bros, made sure he was positioned right next to the blonde who had been giving him the fuck-me eyes.

"So," she said, her red lips curving up into a smile. "Are you a Ranger too?"

"No ma'am," he replied, flashing her a grin. "I'm afraid my job isn't as glamorous as these guys."

"He's only one of the head honchos at the mines," Gabriel said.

"Oh, really?" She turned back to him. "I'm Melanie."

"Nathan," he said. "And I'm not the head honcho. I just make sure all the machines run."

Melanie sidled up closer to him. "Sounds interesting."

Nathan's enhanced sense of smell detected a hint of feathers. *Hmmm. Flight shifter.* He'd never met a female flight shifter before. "Nah, not that interesting. What do you do?"

"I work as a hostess at the French restaurant in town."

"Nice," Gabriel said. "*You* must have interesting stories then. Care to share any?"

"Well, there was that time we caught one of our sous chefs in the freezer with a bus boy ..."

Nathan nodded as Melanie told some hilarious story, laughing at the same time as everyone else. He was good at this—pretending to listen and making her think she was the most interesting thing in the world. How many times had he done it to get into some girl's pants? Too many to count. And Melanie was falling for it, based on how close she was sidling up to him and how she would touch his bicep or his shoulder to grab his attention.

He glanced at his companions. It looked like they weren't doing so bad. Gabriel had his arm around the brunette, and Anders and Daniel were both deep in conversation with the remaining two women.

"So, what do you say we get out of here?" Melanie whispered into his ear.

"Sure," he said automatically. Normally his wolf would have howled in approval at the conquest, but he didn't hear a peep this time. He shrugged it off. "You got a place of your own? If not, we could go to mine and I could drive you home after."

He thought that would have turned her off, but she nodded. "I have my own ride. Let's go."

They didn't bother saying goodbye to everyone though he knew they were all watching as they left. He glanced back and saw Gabriel giving him a wink as he pulled the brunette closer.

Nathan pushed the door open with one hand and let Melanie out first. As the door closed behind them, he stopped short.

Melanie cocked her head at him. "You okay?"

Something didn't feel right. It wasn't Melanie, though. It was him. "Yeah. Listen, Melanie," he began, placing a hand on her shoulder. "I'm just … I have an early day tomorrow."

She chuckled. "Guys usually say that *after*."

"Yeah, well, don't get me wrong. You're gorgeous, and I would be happy to hop into bed with you."

Melanie's eyes narrowed. "But?"

"I'm just tired." Tired of everything. Tired of the same shit over and over again. "Sorry."

"Nah, it's fine." She yawned. "I'm actually pretty exhausted myself. I usually spend my nights off from the restaurant sleeping at home or visiting my sister over in Verona Mills. I only came because my friends wanted to." She looked up at him. "But if you change your mind, I'm always up for a bit of fun."

"Yeah, sure." He jerked a thumb back at The Den. "I'm usually here if I'm looking for some friendly company."

"Great." She fished in her purse for her keys, then held them out triumphantly. "So, I'll see you around?"

"See ya." He watched her walk to the row of cars parked to the left of the door. "Wait!"

Melanie whipped her head around. "Change your mind?"

"No. I mean," he scratched his head, thinking of a way to say it to say it delicately, "can I ask you for a favor?"

"Sure."

"If anyone asks, don't tell them I didn't take you home with me."

She laughed. "Fine. But you *owe* me one."

Nathan breathed a sigh of relief. "You can collect any time."

"I'll hold you to that!"

With a wave of her hand, she walked toward the Honda parked at the end of the row. He watched her get into her car and drive away.

Grabbing his keys out of his pocket, he strode to his parking spot. The shiny yellow vintage Mustang with a black stripe down the middle looked out of place among the pickup trucks and Jeeps, not just in the parking lot, but anywhere he went in town. But he didn't care. He and his dad spent the last couple of years searching for this car and then restoring it to its former glory. The hours tinkering around the garage with his old man, just shooting the shit and drinking beers after a hard day's work, were some of the best times of his life. It was his prized possession and not just because of the value of the restored car. His missed his old man and his ma, but they had recently retired and were now on a well-deserved trip around the world with their friends.

The engine roared to life as he turned the key in the ignition. He shook his head and chuckled. *Maybe I'm just getting old.* He was almost thirty after all, but still a little too young to be having a midlife crisis.

Nathan placed his hands on the wheel, wondering if he'd made a mistake. Melanie was gorgeous and willing and didn't want anything with strings attached. Should he go after her? He bet he could catch up with her if he gunned it.

A voice inside his head told him it was time to go. Time to go home to his dark, lonely apartment.

He squashed those thoughts and put the car in gear. *I'm just tired.*

Nathan threw the wrench he was clenching in his hand, the metal making a loud clanging sound that echoed through the cave. He wiped a greasy palm down his pants. He was not having a good morning. First, one of their smelting machines had broken down and it took hours to get it back up. Then, he found out they were going to have to relocate the next site as it had not contained as much blackstone as they thought. Months of planning down the drain. They would have to work double-time since they were now behind in their production schedule. And now *this*.

"And if you leave this machine on again while you take your break, I'm gonna tear you limb from limb and piss on what's left!" Nathan roared.

"Y-y-yes sir, Mr. Caldwell," Bryce Jenkins said as he cowered.

The smell of fear from the other man was unmistakable, and his fox was crouching in terror. But Nathan didn't give a shit. He hated it when people disrespected machines, especially the ones under his care. Carelessness could cause accidents, not to mention lives. And Lennox Corp., who owned the Blackstone mines, always put the safety of their people above everything else which meant *he* was the one responsible for making sure the equipment ran smoothly and didn't kill anyone.

"Get out!" he snarled.

"S-s-sir?" Bryce stuttered. "Am I fired?"

"No!" He couldn't unilaterally make that decision of course; besides, he knew Bryce would probably never do it again. The younger man was inexperienced, not stupid. "Just get out of my face for now."

"Y-y-yes sir!" Bryce backed up slowly. When he'd put enough distance between them, he turned and scampered away.

"Fuck my life," he said aloud. He gritted his teeth. Someone getting hurt would be the perfect icing for this shit cake of a day. He had to talk to Ben.

Nathan marched out of the cave, deciding to check if Ben was in his office. He immediately spotted Ben and Penny, hand-in-hand, heading to the group of trailers around the main parking lot. He jogged toward them, picking up his pace.

"Ben! Goddamnit Ben, wait up!" He ran faster. "That fucker Jenkins left the fucking grinding machine on again during his break! I told him I was going to tear him limb from limb and piss on whatever was left if he ever—"

Nathan didn't notice the third person with them until he was much closer. Gravel skidded around his work boots as he tried to prevent his momentum from crashing into her, causing him to stop centimeters away.

A sweet scent, like golden honey with an underlying tinge of fur, assaulted his nostrils. He didn't mind; after all, he had a sweet tooth. He stared at the person—no, the woman—in front of him. A gorgeous heart-shaped face. Smooth skin that would surely be soft to touch. Thick, dark hair in a neat bun he longed to set free. Light blue eyes tinged with a darker color along the edges. And they were staring right back at him.

Mine, his wolf growled.

And he felt her animal—whatever it was—roar it right back.

The woman's nostrils flared and her pupils dilated. His spine stiffened, and a growl escaped from his throat.

Shit. This was her. His *mate.*

His brain started turning after what seemed like an eternity. Mate? Him? No, that couldn't be right. He didn't want a mate. He was not ready to settle down yet.

"Oh."

"Oh?" *Was she so stunned that she was speechless?*

"Oh. No." She shook her head. "This simply won't do." Her voice was low and husky with a rich timbre that washed over him like a lover's caress.

"Huh?"

"No, this won't do at all." She gave him a quick once-over, then straightened her shoulders. "I appreciate you and your wolf's interest, but I'm afraid I can't have a mate at this time. So, thank you, and I wish you well."

What. The. Ever. Living. Fuck.

The woman turned to Ben. "Mr. Walker, could we get on with the interview, please? It was a long flight, and I'd really like to go back to my hotel and rest."

Ben was looking at Nathan, his eyes wide. Penny had to elbow him to get his attention. "What? Oh yeah. Penny, sweetheart, could you show Dr. Robichaux to my office? I need to talk to Nathan."

"Of course," Penny said with a nod, and the two women began to walk in the direction of Ben's office.

"Nathan?" Ben began, his voice unsure. "You okay man? Is she your—"

"No way," Nathan said.

"Look, man, I know how it feels when you think your mate is rejecting you, but—"

"You heard her. She doesn't want a mate."

"So? If she's yours—"

"Newsflash Ben: I don't want her either. You think I want a mate?" He let out a laugh, not caring if it sounded forced. "I'm drowning in so much pussy, especially now that you and Jason are off the market. I can have any girl I want. Why would I give that up for some chick?"

"Nathan, you can't stop fate—"

"Don't, Ben. Just don't." He turned around, kicking a rock in his path and shoving his hands into his pockets as he walked away.

Mate? Fuck that. Who the hell needed a mate when freedom was much sweeter?

Besides, she wasn't *that* pretty. She seemed cold and unfeeling. And what was she wearing? She looked out of place wearing a white suit and stiletto heels in the mountains. What kind of interview was she doing with Ben?

His wolf snarled in jealousy thinking of her and Ben alone in his office. *Stupid wolf.* "For fuck's sake, Ben would cut his own balls off before he cheated on Penny," he told his animal.

"Mr. Caldwell, sir!"

He stopped in his tracks and turned around. It was Morris, the smelting room supervisor. Based on the man's face, he wasn't bearing good news.

"What is it?"

"You need to come see this, sir."

Nathan groaned inwardly. He pushed aside thoughts of honey and fur and light blue eyes. "Fine. Show me what's wrong *now*."

CHAPTER TWO

Violet Robichaux was sitting on the chair in front of the large oak desk waiting patiently for Benjamin Walker to come inside to start the interview.

Mine, her tiger hissed. *Mine.*

So that foul-mouthed man—wolf—was supposedly her mate?

Those really existed?

Violet didn't have any shifter peers in the New Orleans neighborhood where she grew up. She had a *normal* upbringing, which her parents had strived to give her. They weren't mates either; they had explained they chose each other because their personalities were suitable. They had similar goals, and it didn't hurt that they were both shifters *and* scientists. Her father was a chemist and her mother was a botanist. Of course, had one of them been a geneticist, perhaps they wouldn't have thought they were so compatible. Recessive genes, after all, had higher chances of mutations, which her own animal certainly was.

Mine, it insisted, interrupting her reverie.

"Oh hush," she said aloud. "I *told* you this can't happen. Not now."

It growled unhappily, but she pushed it away deep inside her so she didn't have to listen to it whine. She wouldn't have gotten this far in her career if she gave in to her animal's demands all the time. Science required discipline and dedication. Her parents, who were also at the forefront of their own fields, taught her that. It was hard enough for a woman in STEM to get ahead, but a shifter, too? She'd learned to hide that part of her over the years by controlling her inner animal.

And now it seemed to want to break free. All for a wolf. The irony.

She supposed he was attractive in that conventional bad boy kind of way, but he wasn't her usual type. Like most shifters he was tall and built like a bodybuilder, though he looked like someone who liked to work outdoors and with his hands. The way his white shirt clung to his broad shoulders and chest was practically obscene. And his dark blond hair was a tad too long, although she wondered what they would feel like between her fingers—

The sound of someone clearing their throat jolted her out of her thoughts. "Dr. Robichaux?" Ben Walker said as he walked through the door. "Sorry to keep you waiting. I had to see my wife off."

"Not a problem."

He sat on the worn leather chair behind the desk. "You said you had a long flight? From where?"

She rolled her eyes inwardly. *Small talk?* She didn't have time for this. "London."

He scratched his head. "Dr. Philipps said you'd been

working abroad for six months, but I could have sworn it wasn't London."

She gave him a tight smile. "No, I've been living in Eritana."

"Eri—wha?"

"It's a small country in the Caucuses, north of Azerbaijan."

"And what were you doing there?"

"I was doing research on the properties of the minerals found in the Vaisjaani Nature Reserves," she said smoothly.

"Sounds, er, interesting."

She smirked. "Yes, it was fascinating."

"So why did you leave?"

"We ran out of funding," she said. It was close enough to the truth. Hopefully he didn't notice the white lie because she had a feeling that despite his hulking size, Ben Walker wasn't a dumb oaf.

"I see." He picked up a folder on his desk. "Well, I've read through the resume Dr. Philipps forwarded to me. He's done nothing but sing praises about you. But tell me: why would you want to be our Chief Geologist?"

Violet sighed and her shoulders sagged. This was an amazing opportunity. She would get to study blackstone, the hardest substance on Earth which could only be mined by dragon fire. Anyone in her field would have given their right arm for this and she had been flattered that her mentor, Dr. Scott Philipps, had chosen her as his replacement. But she wished the timing were better.

"Dr. Robichaux?"

"Right." She cleared her throat delicately. "Mr. Walker—"

"Ben, please."

"All right. Ben. This job would be excellent for my career. I've always been fascinated with the properties of blackstone ever since Dr. Philipps brought a sample to class. So, when he told me about this job a few weeks ago, I jumped at the chance. But I also need to be honest with you. Something came up, and I'm still waiting on another opportunity."

"And what's that?"

She cleared her throat. "I'm trying to secure funding to further my research back in Eritania. I've left a few things undone. I'm afraid I won't be able to accept any position at the moment." She stood up. "My flight was already booked, so I thought I'd come anyway. My apologies for wasting your time."

"Wait." Ben got to his feet and raised a hand. "I mean, please stay, Dr. Robichaux, and hear me out."

Huh? Curiosity pricked at her. "All right." She sat back down and crossed a leg over her knee.

"Dr. Philipps has been with us for almost twenty years now, and he's a well-respected part of our team. We're sad to see him go, but of course he deserves to retire. As you know the position is highly specialized, but aside from the skill and knowledge we also need someone who would fit in around here. With our people."

"Oh." He meant shifters, of course. She knew the prejudices they faced.

"I know Dr. Philipps really wants to get on with his retirement, and I hate to keep him here. So how about this: why don't you fill in temporarily until we can find someone else?"

"Really? You'd let me stay knowing I could leave any moment?"

"Why not? I'll give you a full six months' salary, plus housing and all the benefits if you can stay and help us with the transition. I mean who knows, you might like it here and decide to stay."

She highly doubted that but bit her tongue. A whole six

months' salary for a few weeks of work? If she secured her funding for the year, that additional money could keep her going for another couple of months. Plus she could see them mine the blackstone. She would be stupid to refuse.

"That's very generous of you. Are you sure?"

"Oh, I'm very sure."

There was this ... glint in Ben Walker's eye. Was this some kind of trick?

Take it, the logical voice inside her said. The salary was pocket change to Lennox Corporation but would mean all the world to her.

"All right. That sounds reasonable. I also know a few people who might be a good fit." If she helped them find a replacement, she could leave Blackstone right away and have money to go back to Eritania. This was the perfect solution.

"I'll have HR draw up the papers. Are you staying in town?"

"At the Blackstone Hotel," she said.

Ben nodded. "You can keep staying there while you're here or move into one of our corporate apartments. Just let Janice in HR know what you'd like, and she'll take care of it for you."

"That sounds excellent."

"Can you start tomorrow?"

"Of course," she said.

"Good. You'll be working with our Chief Engineer, Nathan Caldwell. He works with Dr. Philipps closely." He paused. "Is that okay?"

She shrugged. If this Nathan Caldwell worked with Dr. Philipps, she was sure he would be a fine colleague. "That's fine."

Ben's face lit up. "Great."

She stood up. "If you don't mind, I'd like to get some rest."

"Of course. Just call if you need anything else. And, uh …"
He looked at her outfit.

"Don't worry. I have some appropriate work clothes." She
was used to digging in the dirt after all. But, since today was a
formal interview, she wanted to look nice.

"Good. You'll be doing a lot of work inside the mines, so
you should wear some sturdy shoes."

"I will. Thank you again, I'll see myself out." With a final
nod, she pivoted on her heels and headed out the door.

As she walked to her car, Violet still couldn't believe what
had happened. She was going to be working with blackstone
of all things, making a generous salary, and she could walk
away anytime she wanted? Maybe Ben Walker wasn't as smart
as he looked or there was something in the mountain air that
was rotting his brain.

A scent in the air caught her attention. It was male, spicy,
and smelled so good her knees buckled.

Mine!

"Stop!" She was glad no one was around. It must have been
her imagination, or her hyper senses picking up the lingering
scent. "He is *not* ours. Didn't you hear what he said?"

If her sense of smell was good, her hearing was even
better.

Newsflash Ben: I don't want her either.

You think I want a mate?

I'm drowning in so much—

Jealous growls silenced her thoughts.

"You're being unreasonable." She yanked open the door of
her rented car. "And I can't believe I'm even talking to you."

Violet slid into the front seat and shoved the key into the
ignition. A deep breath escaped her lips.

"He's not interested. He's far too busy entertaining other

women." The angry snarl was something she'd never heard before, especially not from her own mouth.

"No, we have to forget about him." She closed her eyes. "Remember why we're here. So we can go back. *Remember.*"

Her tiger quieted down as her own chest tightened with pain.

"Now, let's focus."

When she didn't hear any more protests, she turned the key and drove back to her hotel.

CHAPTER THREE

NATHAN PULLED his car into his parking space and cut the engine before yanking the keys and shoving them into his pocket. He shouldn't have gone home, but he needed a shower and his own bed after nearly eight hours of overtime trying to get the damn smelter to work.

As a shifter, he didn't need a lot of sleep ... if his wolf was cooperating.

Mine, it whined. *Mine.*

His inner wolf wasn't letting go. It was angry at him, seething and gnashing its teeth, refusing to give him a moment of peace. Even other shifters seemed wary of him. Yesterday, he nearly broke a wrench in half because he was so distracted.

"She's gone," he said. Well, she must be by now. She wasn't from around here based on how she dressed, even though she was definitely a shifter. What was she, anyway? Feline, he was sure. Wolves had the best sense of smell out of all shifters, but he'd never smelled anyone like her.

He had to get her out of his mind. Maybe then his damn wolf would forget her and move on. With an unhappy sigh, he got out of the car and headed for the mouth of the cave.

Nathan's office was inside the mine itself, in a small trailer they moved around depending on where the current vein was located. He shared it with their geologist, Dr. Philipps, whose work was valuable not only in finding bigger veins, but also in researching the properties of blackstone. Thanks to him, they were able to patent about a dozen more uses for the material which led to larger profits for Lennox. He would be sad to see Doc Philipps go, but he supposed the man needed to retire eventually. Hopefully whoever they got to replace him wouldn't be a prick.

He grabbed the safety helmet, goggles, and vest from the security guard and walked into the mine, all the way to his trailer just off the main cavern. The lights were already on, but he wasn't surprised. Dr. Philipps was usually there before him, even on normal days.

"Hey, Doc," he greeted as he stepped inside. "How are—"

The familiar scent of golden honey and fur hit his nostrils nearly knocking him back. His wolf perked up happily, knowing who was nearby. "What the fuck?"

Three sets of eyes stared back at him. Ben. Doc Philipps. And her. Her and those damn eerily beautiful eyes.

"Oh." Her plump pink lips parted.

Oh? Is that all she knew how to say?

"Nathan!" Dr. Philipps greeted. "Good, you're here. I want you to meet Dr. Violet Robichaux, a former student of mine. Violet, this is Nathan Caldwell, our Chief Engineer."

Violet turned to Ben. "*This* is Nathan Caldwell?"

Ben gave her an innocent look. "Yes. I did ask if you were okay working with him."

Her mouth dropped open and her nostrils flared. "You didn't—"

"Wait. What the hell is going on here?" Nathan asked.

"That's what I was trying to explain," the Doc said. "Violet is here as my replacement."

"What?" Nathan's head whipped to Violet and then to Ben. "You're hiring *her*? To work *here*?"

"Temporarily," she clarified. "I'll only be taking the job on an interim basis since Dr. Philipps will be leaving within the week."

Dr. Philipps took off his glasses. "I really was hoping you'd take the job which is why I already sold my house and made my travel arrangements to see my sister in Florida. But I understand things change and you've got more exciting opportunities on the horizon. I am grateful you're willing to stay and help until they find a permanent replacement. Are you sure I can't convince you to change your mind?"

"I'm flattered you chose me, Dr. Philipps, but I'm afraid I can't stay *here*."

Her pert little nose wrinkled like she had smelled something distasteful. Seriously? Blackstone wasn't glamorous or exciting, but it was his home. So she was one of those women who preferred life in the big city. *Good riddance, then*. He couldn't wait for her to leave. His wolf growled in protest, but he ignored it.

Ben cleared his throat. "Say, Nathan, maybe you and the doc can show Violet around the mines? Give her a quick tour."

"I'm busy." He walked over to his desk on the right side of the office. "I have actual work to do today. You know, after staying here until three a.m. to make sure that damn smelter didn't kill anyone."

"I'll be happy to give her the tour myself," Dr. Philipps said.

"Thank you," she replied. "I've been looking forward to this." Ignoring Nathan, she turned to Ben. "I'll see you later, Ben."

Dr. Philipps led Violet out of the trailer and as soon as the door closed behind them, Nathan shot to his feet. "Really, Ben? *Really*?"

"What?" he said in an innocent voice.

"Don't give me those teddy bear eyes; they only work on women and children." He picked up the closest thing he could —a box of pencils—and threw it against the wall in anger. "Why *her*?"

"Because she's smart and qualified? Look, this has been in the works way before you met her. The doc recommended her the moment he told me he was retiring. That was weeks ago."

"Yeah but …" What could he say?

"Are you going to have a problem working with her? Because she said—"

"No, damn you," he cursed. "It'll be fine. I'll be fine. I can handle it." He sank down on his chair. "Besides, she's just here for a couple of weeks. She probably won't have to do anything major in that time."

"Yeah, she'll be collecting the samples, doing the testing, sending them to the lab for further analysis. Just the day-to-day stuff he usually does."

"Good." He turned his computer on so forcefully, his thumb nearly pushed the button in. When Ben snickered, he glared back at him. "Is there anything else?"

"What? Oh nothing. I was just thinkin' you know." He shook his head. "I hope Violet doesn't cause a scene out there with our guys … with her being the only female out on the floor and a shifter, too." He chuckled.

Nathan shot to his feet so fast, the monitor shook and the table moved forward a couple of inches. "Fuck," he muttered under his breath.

"You okay, buddy?"

"Yeah, I'm fine." He walked around his table and toward the door.

"Where are you going?"

He grabbed the extra vest and helmet they kept in the office. "She didn't have any damn safety gear on. I better make sure she gets this."

"It's fine. She's a shifter and—"

"Rules are rules," Nathan said as he jerked the door open. He wasn't lying. Even though shifters could heal faster and survive most things that could kill a human, they still wore safety gear inside the mines.

"But what—"

He slammed the door to drown out Ben's voice. *I just want to make sure she doesn't get injured,* he told himself. Yeah. That was it.

Violet was actually wearing more appropriate clothes today, at least from what he could remember. He was too busy staring at her face and then trying not to stare at her to notice.

Where could they be? The cavern they dug out to mine this section was humongous with several tunnels that led to the other parts. She was a geologist and said she was looking forward to this tour, so he guessed she'd want to see the main vein and headed there.

He was right. Violet and Dr. Philipps were standing in the cavern, chatting softly and inspecting the walls. And, as Ben had predicted, the sharks were already circling. A group of their workers were idling by the maintenance carts, staring at Violet and Dr. Philipps and elbowing each other like teenagers.

Nathan's hands curled into fists, and his wolf gnashed its teeth. "Get back to work," he barked at them, startling a few of the men. Even from this distance, they were still way too close to Violet.

"Er, yes sir," Cody, one of the newer hires, said with an audible gulp. He turned tail and strode away with the rest following his example. The tightness in his chest loosened when they disappeared through the tunnel that led to the outside.

They could have at least pretended to work, he thought as he marched toward the two geologists.

"... And as you can see, the blackstone is really embedded in the *nitride londaleite*, and nothing can get it out—Oh." He stopped when Nathan approached them. "Nathan, did you need something?"

Violet whipped around, her eyes narrowing at him.

He held out the vest and helmet. "Here. You forgot to put this on."

"I don't need it."

"Yeah, you do if you wanna work here. Everyone here has to wear it," Nathan insisted, then gestured at himself and Dr. Philipps. "Both shifters and humans. It makes it easier for everyone."

She let out a huff. "Fine." Grabbing the gear from him, she began to put it on.

Nathan could ignore how the curves of her breasts stretched against her t-shirt or even the way her jeans seemed to mold to her ass. But when she took out the clip that held her bun in place so the hat could fit more comfortably, he couldn't stop the groan that left his mouth. Her dark hair tumbled down her shoulders, sending another gust of her scent his way.

"Nathan?" she asked in that low, husky voice of hers. "Are you all right?"

Fuck, he never thought someone's smell and the sound of their voice could arouse him, but Violet saying his name had him hard as steel in a second. Thank God for the vest covering his erection. He cleared his throat. "Yeah, I'm fine."

"Glad you decided to join us," Dr. Philipps said. "This should make things easier. I won't be putting you to work today, Violet, but you should at least have an idea of how things run around here. Nathan can answer any questions you have that I might not be able to."

"Right," she said. "Okay, let's continue then."

"Why don't you keep going, Doc?" Nathan said. "You've been working here since I was a teenager. I'll just pipe in if I need to add anything."

"As you wish. Let's head to the smelting room."

Nathan followed behind them, keeping close to Violet. He tensed the moment they walked into the busy room as every pair of eyes zeroed in on her. He sent them a nasty glare which had everyone looking away except for one or two of the cockier bastards. He made a mental note of who they were. Maneuvering himself beside her, he made sure she wasn't in anyone's line of sight for the rest of the time.

This is fucking insane. But his wolf wouldn't leave him alone. Violet sent him a curious stare, those strange eyes luminous even in the low light. Again, he was itching to know. What was she? He couldn't sense her animal again, but she was probably one of those who kept a tight rein on their shifter side.

He hated to admit it, but what was bothering him the most was how cold and unfeeling she acted. He and his wolf were going crazy, and he could barely keep his anger and lust in check while she seemed unfazed by the whole thing. Like yesterday had never happened and everything was hunky-dory and normal. Her face remained passive, barely defying any emotion. Did she ever flinch or break?

Finally, the damn tour was almost over. He was getting tired of gritting his teeth and glaring at every single male who glanced their way.

"I'm going to grab those samples I told you about," Dr. Philipps said as they stood in front of the trailer. "As you've seen, I've cleaned up my desk so feel free to poke around and unpack as you wish."

"Thank you, Dr. Philipps."

"You're welcome." The older man walked away leaving them alone.

"Excuse me," she began.

"Yes?"

"I mean," she gestured to the door, "kindly move aside so I can get into my office."

"You mean our office," he corrected.

"Right." She crossed her arms over her chest, but he didn't move. "Is there a problem?"

"So, what are you?"

"I beg your pardon?"

"I don't know what you are. Big cat, right? But," Nathan leaned in and took a whiff, "what kind?"

The look she gave him would have frozen a lesser man. "That's rather forward." She moved around him and disappeared into the doorway.

"Lioness? Panther?" he asked as he followed her inside. "Am I getting close?"

She huffed and ignored him, walking to the empty table on the left side instead.

"C'mon," he said. "Or do you wanna show me instead? I'd love to see your pussy—"

"I *beg* your pardon!"

"--*cat*," he continued. Her hair had whipped around her, surrounding her pretty face like a dark halo. Those light eyes blazed with anger. *Finally a reaction.* He grinned at her. "Jeez. You gotta let me finish my sentence if we're going to be working together."

"Temporarily," she said in a firm voice.

Before she could say anything else, the door flew open.

"So, how was the tour?" Ben flashed him a knowing smile. That bastard.

"It was interesting," Violet said. "Fascinating really. Aside from seeing the process from beginning to end, I would love to know more about the history of the mine."

"Matthew and Jason can tell you more about that," Ben said. "You'll meet them tomorrow at the company picnic."

"Shit, that's tomorrow?" Nathan ran his fingers through his hair. He had totally forgotten.

Violet shook her head. "I'm sure I could speak with them in a more professional environment. Dr. Philipps explained that they come here every couple of days or so, correct?"

"Yeah, sure." Ben scratched his chin with his thumb and forefinger. "But you know, the company picnic's a lot of fun. We have a big party by the lake with slides and bouncy castles and games for the kids. Lots of good food, too. And, it's actually going to be Doc's retirement party. You can't miss that."

CHAPTER FOUR

*I*T *WAS the sound of shuffling feet and hushed masculine voices that shook her awake.*

Those sounds were unusual, not only in the middle of the night, but also up in the mountains. Here, where there were few modern conveniences, Violet could only hear the breeze or the chirping of the birds in the evening. Or, when she tuned in using her enhanced hearing, a cow mooing sadly in the distance or a rabbit rustling under some bushes, digging around for its next meal.

And of course, the laughter and cheer of the children—the little girls—living in the compound where she stayed.

Her tiger raised its hackles, and Violet shot to her feet. Instinct kicked in. Danger, it said. As she exited her tent, little did she know she wouldn't be hearing laughter again ...

Violet's eyes flew open, her heart beating in her chest like a drum. The sheets were stuck to her skin, the sweat making it slick. *It was a dream.* At least, today it was.

She sat up and took a deep breath, then got up and walked to the window. The early morning light filled the room and from her hotel, the view of the Blackstone Mountains was magnificent. She should feel grateful to be here. But instead she only felt guilt. It was supposed to be the start of her new career. Then, it happened.

Violet shut the drapes closed, the room going dark. She just had to make it through the next few weeks. Then the funding would come in and she could go back to what she had left behind. She checked her email; no news yet. Not from the university and not from Antonia back in Eritana. No news should be good news, she supposed.

Checking the clock by the bedside, she realized it was nearly eight a.m. Ben said they'd stop by around eighty-thirty, so she had to get ready now.

Violet showered and put on a pair of khaki shorts, a black tank top, and flip-flops. She didn't have much nice clothing; most of the stuff she had was functional and her nicer clothes were in storage back in New Orleans. The shoes and suit she was wearing for her interview the other day had been bought off-the-rack when she got to Colorado.

This will have to do, she thought as she looked at herself in the mirror. *Why did I even agree to go?* She could have argued she didn't have anything to wear, or she was far too jet lagged. But when Ben said it was also Dr. Philipps' retirement party, she couldn't very well have said no.

To say she was shocked when Nathan walked into the office was an understatement. She wanted to quit on the spot. Ben did tell her she would be working with their Chief Engineer, but not who he was. Did Ben know? Probably, but she couldn't prove it.

It was a good thing she was used to being in control, of her animal and of herself. She was determined to ignore him and treat him with cold, professional indifference.

And that cad. The way he teased her and asked about her animal. It was rude and unprofessional. Exactly what she expected from a crude wolf like him. Who cared if he was handsome as sin and his smile made her feel warm all over? And the way he said he wanted to see her—

Mine, came the satisfied purr from her throat.

She laid a hand on her chest in surprise. "Shush!" Her tiger had never done that before, not with any man she had met or dated. "We can't do this. Remember why. *Remember.*" She shut her eyes, the vision in her head clear as day.

And then silence from her tiger.

She had to stay focused and couldn't afford any distractions. And Nathan Caldwell was certainly the biggest distraction of them all.

After brushing her long dark hair and tying it up with a rubber band, she grabbed her bag and headed downstairs.

As she exited the elevator, she saw Ben and his wife waiting in the lobby. They seemed a mismatched couple—with Ben being so tall and Hulk-like and Penny so small and delicate like a china doll. But even Violet could see they adored each other.

He had his arm around her protectively and leaned down to whisper something in her ear that made her face as red as her hair. The way he looked at her, it was like there was no one else in the room.

"Violet," Penny greeted as she approached them. "You look nice."

"Thank you," she replied. "I hope I didn't keep you waiting too long."

"Not at all," Ben said. "It's going to about a two hour drive to the picnic site. We can stop and get coffee and breakfast to go if you want, though I'd save some room." He chuckled, patting his stomach. "Lennox tends to overdo these things and there'll be lots of food and drink throughout the day."

"That's fine." She followed them outside, where Ben led them to the large black Jeep parked by the door.

"Wait," Ben said as he opened front passenger-side door for his wife.

"Ben," Penny said with a giggle as he picked her up and put her into the front seat. "I told you, I'm fine."

"But you might slip and fall, and I'd never forgive myself." His large hand went to stomach.

Ah, so Penny was carrying a cub. It was normal, then, for Ben to be protective.

As Ben turned to Violet, she put her hands up. "I'm fine. I can get up on my own."

Ben chuckled. "I wasn't going to offer." He did, however, open the door for her.

"Thank you," she said and climbed inside.

They drove out of town and up the highway that led to the mines, but after a couple of miles they veered off to the east side where the road forked. Ben explained the lake was actually in the valley in the middle of the mountains, and they would be driving for another hour to get there. They stopped to fill up on gas, and Violet and Penny went into the little convenience store to grab coffee and snacks.

An hour later, Ben pulled off on a side road covered with a thick canopy of trees. Violet wondered if they were going to the right place, but a few seconds later, the Jeep pulled onto a dirt road that led to a large clearing.

"It's beautiful," Penny said as they drove closer to the shore.

Ben looked up ahead. "I shouldn't have waited so long to

bring you out here, but the weather hasn't exactly been great until now."

Violet stared out the window at the breathtaking sight. It was gorgeous—the green mountains surrounded the sparkling waters of the lake. There was already a large crowd there—men, women, and children—swimming, kayaking, playing on the giant bouncy castle, or just sunning themselves on the sand.

The blue skies seemed endless, and it was like the puffs of white clouds dotting the horizon had been hand-painted by an artist. She squinted as she saw a bird flying in the distance. No, wait. What in God's name was *that*? A hawk? An eagle? It was much too large to be any of those.

As the figure came closer, Violet realized how gigantic it was. The dragon was twenty—no, fifty—feet tall. The golden scales that covered its body glinted in the sun, and the wing-span of its bat-like wings was twice its height. She couldn't help it and let out a gasp.

"Is that—"

Penny and Ben looked at each other. "Jason," they said in unison.

Ben pulled the Jeep into an empty spot in the makeshift parking lot by the tree line. As they headed to the shore, the dragon flew overhead in circles before landing. The earth shook as its enormous clawed feet dropped to the ground.

"Let's go say hi."

Violet's natural instincts kicked in as they drew closer. The dragon was massive and dominant, and her tiger cowed and became uneasy. *Calm down*, she told the tiger. It was normal, of course. The dragon was Alpha around here, and she was a stranger in its territory.

The dragon began to shrink, and the scales disappeared

into human skin. As it reduced in size, a blonde woman ran up and tossed it some clothes. Human hands caught it.

"Show off." The woman smirked as she came up to the man who was now hopping into swim shorts.

He wrapped an arm around her waist and pulled her close, then gave her a quick kiss. "You know I do it for the kids," he said with a grin.

Indeed most of the children had stopped what they were doing and stared at him. When he waved at them, they all cheered. With dragons being so rare, Violet imagined this was a treat for them to see such a creature up close.

"Hey Penny, Ben," the blonde woman greeted.

"Christina, Jason." Penny waved at them, then gestured to Violet. "This is Dr. Violet Robichaux. Violet, this is Jason and Christina Lennox."

"How do you do?" She held out her hand.

"Nice to meet you, Dr. Robichaux," Christina said, shaking it.

Human, she sensed. "Please, call me Violet."

"You're Dr. Philipps' replacement," Jason said.

"Temporarily." When he gave her a blank look, she frowned. Maybe he wasn't involved in the day-to-day stuff, but still, she would have thought the position of Chief Geologist would have been important enough to him to know the details.

"Er, I'll explain later," Ben said quickly. "Where's Matthew? He didn't feel like putting on a show like you?"

Jason jerked his finger behind him. "Over there, of course, with Catherine."

"You should meet him, too," Ben said to Violet.

They walked over to the group of people chatting as they stood around a table laden with snacks and drinks. As they came closer, Violet did a double take. The man and woman standing in the circle of people looked exactly like Jason and Christina.

"You're not going crazy," Penny laughed. "Matthew and Jason are identical twins and so are their mates."

"Mates?"

Penny nodded. "Yup. Crazy, huh?"

Crazy indeed.

They approached the couple and Violet was introduced to them, plus a few other people from Lennox Corp.

"Oh, so you're replacing Dr. Philipps?" Matthew said.

"Tempora—"

"Penny, sweetheart," Ben interrupted. "I think I see Sybil and Kate over by that table. Didn't you say you needed to talk to them? Maybe you can introduce Violet."

"Huh? Uh, yeah, sure. Let's go Violet."

Hmm, that seemed rude, Violet thought. After all, Matthew was the CEO. "I was hoping to ask Mr. Lennox more about the mountains."

"Well, if you want to know more about the history of Blackstone and the Lennoxes, you can ask Sybil," Ben offered. "She's Matthew and Jason's sister, and she knows everything about the mines and the town."

"The female dragon, right?" she said. Though she didn't keep up with shifter news and lore, she knew female dragons were rare.

"Don't worry; she's super nice," Penny said. She grabbed Violet by the elbow. "Let's go."

Violet allowed Penny to lead her away, her mind already whirling with questions for the youngest Lennox dragon.

The two women sitting by themselves at a picnic table looked as different as night and day. The one on the right had dark hair that hung down her back in a braid. She was wearing a one-piece suit and a long skirt that covered her legs. The woman across from her, on the other hand, wore a bright pink bikini that matched the ends of her dark blonde hair. A small nose piercing sparkled in the sun as she turned to them. Why did she look familiar?

"Penny, my girl!" She waved them over.

"I like your new hair and the piercing, Kate," Penny said as she sat down next to her.

"Yeah, I was tired of the old me. I was thinking of getting some ink done, too." She turned to Violet. "Who's this?"

"Oh. This is Dr. Violet Robichaux."

"Vi! I like it!" She stood up. "I'm Kate."

"It's Violet," she corrected.

"But Vi is so much cuter and efficient," Kate said, then pulled her in for a hug. Violet stood there awkwardly, her arms stiff at her sides, unsure of what to do. When she took a deep breath, the scent of fur filled her nostrils. Wolf, definitely. As soon as she felt Kate's limbs loosen, she disentangled herself as fast as she could.

"Er, I suppose so—"

"Great! It's settled then, Vi."

Violet wasn't sure what was settled, but she shrugged it off.

"I'm Sybil Lennox," the other woman said, flashing her a bright smile. With her sweet face and sunny expression, Violet wouldn't have guessed this young woman turned into a giant fire-breathing dragon. "I've never seen you before. Which department do you work at?"

"I'm Dr. Philipps' replacement," Violet said.

Sybil scooted over and motioned for her to sit down beside her. "Ben told me he was retiring. He's such a nice guy;

he's been working for us since I was a little girl. So you'll be Chief Geologist now? That's awesome!"

"Finally, more girls in the mines. Yes!" Kate raised a fist in triumph. "Let's take down the sausage fest. And you're a shifter too, right?" She sniffed at Violet. "You don't smell like any cat I know. What are you? Cougar? Lynx?"

"You work in the mines as well?" Violet asked, quickly changing the subject.

"As a consultant. I don't do the 9-to-5 thing. I like the freedom of freelancing," she said. "I do software for the computer systems there and at Lennox. Unfortunately that moron Chief Engineer couldn't program his way out of a paper bag."

"Excuse me?"

Kate laughed and looked around. "Where is my brother, anyway?"

Brother? Violet looked at the other woman closely. No wonder she seemed familiar. She and Nathan had the same eyes, nose, and chin, though Kate's features were softer.

"Oh, never mind. Of course that's where he is."

Violet's gaze followed where she was looking. There he was. Nathan was standing in the water, beer in hand, wearing only swim shorts. He was surrounded by three women in bikinis, all laughing and giggling as he pretended to splash them.

Mine! The tiger's claws came out. *Mine!*

Shut it!

But Violet's stomach tightened, even as she forced herself to look away. Damn her enhanced hearing. She could make out Nathan's laughs and the girls' cries of *Stop Nathan!* And *You're getting my hair wet, Nathan!* Jealousy began to seep through her veins. She huffed. No, she was going to put her foot down. This was *not* jealousy. Why the hell would she be jealous of those vacuous women?

"Oh brother," Sybil rolled her eyes.

"At least he's not *your* brother," Kate said.

Penny gave Violet a sheepish look, but remained silent.

"I swear, he lets his dick do the thinking all the time."

"Kate!" Penny admonished.

"What? It's true." Kate tossed her hair. "You know he's got a revolving door on his bedroom."

Penny let out a small *eeep!* and went pale.

"Penny!" Sybil exclaimed. "Are you okay?"

"Is it the baby?" Kate reached over and placed a hand on Penny's stomach.

"I ... uh, would you guys mind getting me some water?"

Kate stood up and winked at her. "No prob, mommy. I'll grab a bottle from the table."

"I came prepared with crackers in my cooler!" Sybil got up. "Be back in a sec." The two women walked in opposite directions, leaving Violet and Penny alone.

Penny let out a breath and the color of her face returned to normal. "I'm s-sorry," she said in a quiet voice.

"For what?"

Her eyes lowered. "About what they're saying about Nathan. And just to let you know, I won't be telling anyone what I heard the other day. About you guys being mates."

Violet straightened her shoulders. "First of all, you shouldn't apologize for something that's not your fault. I already knew Nathan was a cad, so it's not news to me." Of course actually seeing it was entirely different, but she swallowed the feeling that was *not* jealousy deep inside. "Second of all, why would Ben ask you not to mention us being mates?"

"Ben told me, but it was Nathan who asked us not to tell anyone."

Violet's nostrils flared, and she felt heat creeping up her neck. Her tiger roared in outrage, furious at its mate's denial.

"Uh, Violet?"

Before she could say anything, Kate and Sybil returned. An indignant shriek caught their attention.

"Nathan! Stop that!"

Nathan and one of the girls were now in the deeper end, and she was pushing him and giggling over God-knows-what he was doing under the water.

Kate turned to Violet. "You'll be working closely with him as Dr. Philipps' replacement, so I apologize in advanced for my brother's actions. He's going to try to get in your pants at some point, but I know you're smart enough to avoid that train wreck."

The words were out of her mouth before she could stop them. "Don't worry, I've already said no. I simply told him I wasn't in need of a mate at the moment."

Shit.

The silence at the table would have been deafening had it not been for the sounds of the picnic around them. Still, Violet's ears were ringing.

That damn tiger.

"Kate, flies are going to go into your mouth," Sybil said in a droll voice.

Kate's jaw shut. "You're. Freaking. Joking." She looked at Penny. "This is a joke, right?"

Penny's red face said it all.

Kate's head turned to Violet. "Oh. My. God." Then she let out a hoot and started laughing.

"So, you're Nathan's mate?" Sybil said. "Like, for real? How did you know?"

Violet straightened her spine. "My animal seemed to recognize him, but I shut that down quickly. Mates and the mating bond have never been scientifically proven. In fact, we already know the so-called mating bond is not a prerequisite for procreation nor can we prove that children born from that bond are superior to offspring of non-mates. My own parents weren't mates as is the case with many shifter couples. It's not a big deal."

"Hold on. So you don't think mates have to end up with each other?" Sybil asked.

"It doesn't make sense. Scientifically," Violet said in her most authoritative voice. "If a species wants to survive, they simply can't wait around for their *supposed* fated mate to show up. Shifters and humans wouldn't have been able to propagate for so many centuries if that were the case. I simply believe that while Nathan and I may be mates, it's not necessary for us to bond and procreate." The argument sounded logical and based on science. But why did she have a strange knot in her stomach?

"My parents weren't mates," Kate said in a sober voice, wiping the tears from her eyes. "But Sybil's were and so are Ben and Penny."

Violet cursed at herself silently, wishing she had known that before she had gone on and on. Her bluntness tended to alienate people, and she was used to it. But for some reason, she didn't want to do that to these women. And she knew she might have, seeing Penny shift in her seat uncomfortably and Sybil's brows draw into a frown.

"I meant no offense," she said to the two women. "Like I said, I'm sure Sybil is a fine specimen, er, woman, and Penny, you'll have a healthy and wonderful child. But, Sybil, you don't consider yourself more superior to me and Kate just because our parents weren't mates, right?"

"Uh, I guess not." The younger woman seemed mollified.

"But Violet," Penny began. "I'm human, but being mates … I can't explain it, but it's just special. Not that I think you're not a great person on your own … or anything. But, aren't you at least curious about what it would be like? It could be wonderful for you too."

Three pairs of eyes stared back at her, waiting for a response. For a brief moment, she thought about it. What it would be like to be held in his arms and kissed by him. But reality washed over her as she remembered his words.

"He agrees with me," she stated.

"So, you've talked with him?" Sybil asked.

"Not exactly. But I overheard him tell Ben he doesn't want a mate." Or rather, he didn't want *her*. The knot in her stomach grew tighter.

"What?" Penny exclaimed. "They were standing twenty feet from us!"

Violet tapped at her earlobe. "Big cat hearing."

"Shit, that sounds like my brother. He's never had a serious relationship." Kate shook her head, but then her lips curled into a smile. "I mean, whatever, right? You guys are free to do what you choose. Fuck fate!"

"Er …" That wouldn't be quite how she would say it.

Sybil and Penny looked dismayed, but said nothing.

Kate looked around. "So, Violet, what do you say we go for a swim?"

Violet shook her head. "I don't think so."

"What? Are kitties like you afraid of the water?" Kate goaded.

Her tiger reared up and bared its fangs as if to say *How dare this wolf say I'm afraid?* "Uh, it's not that. I didn't bring anything appropriate for swimming."

"Oh, you can borrow one of my suits," Sybil offered. "I brought extras."

Kate guffawed. "No thank you; she doesn't need one of those circus tents you call a swimsuit, Sybil." She grabbed something from under the table. "Here. I bought this bikini the other day. It still has tags."

"Thank you, but—"

"Great!" Kate stood up, placed the suit in Violet's hands, and grabbed her by the elbow. "Let's go."

Sybil groaned. "Kate, what are you planning?"

"What?" she asked, an innocent look on her face. "Violet and I are going to get changed. This'll be fun. Trust me."

Violet could hear Sybil and Penny's protests, but she couldn't extricate herself from Kate's firm grasp, not without using her own enhanced strength. She glanced over to the water, where Nathan and that girl had been, but they were gone. At least she didn't have to listen to them anymore. Besides, when was the last time she had gone swimming or even done anything to relax? Too long. The weather was perfect, and the view was phenomenal. She even bet the lake was just the right temperature, and it might prove to be a good distraction for her and her tiger.

"Here you go." Kate shoved her into an empty changing room. "Put this on. I'll be back in a few minutes."

"Where are you going?"

Kate bit her lip as if trying to stop herself from laughing. "To get some popcorn for the show."

"What show?"

"Er, you'll see." The door shut before she could ask Kate any more questions.

CHAPTER FIVE

NATHAN GRABBED another beer from the cooler and popped the tab open, closing his eyes as he drank the ice cold liquid. *Finally, some R and R.* After a shitty week, he just needed to relax and have a couple of beers. He glanced at the three girls —Sherry, Jeannie, and Marjorie—who were sitting on their towels, tanning themselves. They worked in the accounting department at Lennox Corp., which is why he'd never seen them before. The moment he arrived, he started flirting with them as they were in line for the changing rooms. They were very friendly—especially Jeannie—but he couldn't muster anything more than a passing interest.

They're Lennox employees, he told himself. It would be unprofessional to hook up with any of them. And this was a family-oriented event. Surely Matthew and Jason would definitely not approve of him taking some chick out for some fun in the woods.

Yeah, that was it. That was the reason why he didn't try anything else with them. Certainly not because of some uptight geologist who somehow buried herself in his brain so that no matter what he did his every thought seemed to come back to her.

Not at all.

As he took another swig of his beer, his ears perked up when he heard a familiar name.

"Yeah, that Kate Caldwell is fucking hot. I wish she'd come and work on my computer systems," someone laughed.

"She does specialize in *soft*ware, so she could help you with that."

His temple began to throb. *What the fuck.* He turned around slowly.

"Oh man, that bikini she's wearing—Oh shit."

"That bikini she's wearing is *what?*" Nathan asked through gritted teeth.

"Mr. Caldwell, sir, I didn't see you there."

Nathan crossed his arms over his chest. He recognized two of the three men as workers from Lennox. Pencil pushers of some sort. Humans, too. And obviously, they knew who he was.

The one he overheard talking about Kate's bikini took an audible swallow. "Hey, I was just, you know … kidding about what I said earlier."

"Yeah," the other one added. "We weren't looking at your sister or anything."

The last guy laughed. "Besides, that other chick with her is *way* hotter."

"Other chick?" he asked. "What other chick?"

"Er, that one."

Nathan's eyes zeroed in on the figure coming out of the water and slowly heading to the shore.

"Mother*fucker!*" he roared, the beer can in his fist turning into a ball of tin. His wolf reared up and let out an angry growl, baring its teeth.

Violet was wearing the tiniest bikini he'd ever seen. The narrow triangles in front covered her nipples but bared a good amount of cleavage and side boob. The bottom was more modest, but the pale yellow fabric left very little to the imagination, at least for his shifter eyes. She reached up to squeeze the excess water from her hair, pushing her breasts up high, then making them bounce deliciously as she dropped her hands to her sides.

White hot rage shot through him, and he marched toward her with his hands balled into fists at his sides. She was adjusting the side of her bottoms when he stopped in front of her. Goddamn, that thing was even more scandalous up close. Her nipples were poking through the thin stretchy fabric, and he could make out the shadow of a landing strip over her mound. Fuck, he didn't know if he was angry or aroused.

Sensing he was near, her head whipped up. Dark-ringed light eyes grew wide with surprise. "Nathan?"

"What are you doing?"

"I was swimming," she said matter-of-factly.

"I mean, what are you doing here? And what are you wearing?"

She crossed her arms under her breasts, pushing them up farther. "I was invited, remember? And I'm wearing a bathing suit. That's usually what people wear when they go swimming."

Nathan looked around them and saw a discarded towel by his foot. He reached down, grabbed it, and threw it over her shoulders.

She shrieked as sand flew everywhere. "What the hell, Nathan!"

"There, that's much better," he said.

She tossed the towel at him. "That's not mine! What if the owner needs it?"

"Who the fuck cares?" He put it over her again.

A snort from behind made him turn around. Kate was sitting on a beach mat laughing like a hyena and eating from a tub of popcorn by her feet. "Please, keep going," she said with a grin.

"Nathan, what is the matter with you?" Violet asked, hands on her hips.

"What's the matter with me?" he asked in an incredulous voice. *"What's the matter with me?"* Goddamnit, he wished he knew. Without thinking, he grabbed her by the elbow and dragged her away. As they passed by Kate, he kicked sand at her popcorn tub and ignored her cry of "I was eating that, you jerk!"

It wasn't easy as Violet was much stronger than she looked, and she struggled with all her might. He didn't want to bruise her, so, he did the only thing he could think of, which was pick her up and put her over his shoulders.

"Nathan, everyone's looking at us," she hissed. "What will they say?"

"I don't care." He marched them off into the woods, away from everyone, because the entire picnic suddenly felt too crowded. Too loud with too many people, too many men looking at Violet. It was driving him and his wolf crazy.

"Put me down this instant!" she demanded, her fists beating on his back.

"In a minute," he snapped. "We're almost there."

His Mustang was parked in a clearing just off the small path that led to the lake. He spent a lot of time up here with his dad, so they always used this "secret" parking spot. No one knew about it, and he didn't even have to lock the doors when he parked here. When he got to his car, he dropped her to her feet.

Violet staggered back but regained her balance, then brushed her hair away from her face. "What's the meaning of this? Why did you bring me here?"

"You put yourself out there on display and—"

"Excuse me! But how dare you! I'm free to do as I want, whenever I want. I was swimming in a public place, not putting myself out there on display for anyone."

Nathan opened his mouth but shut it quickly. She was right, of course. He was being a jerk. But still, he couldn't help it. It was driving him and his wolf crazy, all those men looking at her, knowing what they were thinking. Because he was thinking the same thing.

He huffed out a breath. "I have some towels in the trunk." He turned away. "You should dry off and we can go—" He stopped when he felt a hand on his bicep. Slowly, he looked back at her.

Violet was staring at him, the pupils of her eyes dilated. As her pink lips parted and her nostrils flared, he smelled the unmistakable scent of golden honey, fur, and arousal.

"Vi—"

She was definitely much stronger than she looked as he nearly tumbled into her when she pulled him close. He put his hands on the hood of his car, trapping her. Violet's damp soft skin and curves felt amazing against him. God, this was so wrong.

"Nathan," she whispered in that sultry voice of hers. And he lost it.

He covered her mouth with his hungrily, and the moment their lips touched it was like fireworks exploded around him.

She moaned, pushing her body up against him. Goddamn, she was as sweet as she smelled, and he could scent how wet she was which made his cock stand at attention. Her arms wound around his neck and pulled him closer, her mouth eagerly moving against his.

He pushed her down, laying on top of her as she splayed out on the hood of his car and planted her heels on the front bumper. She spread her legs, accommodating him between her thighs, brushing up against him and creating a sweet friction that would have had him creaming his pants if he'd been some inexperienced teenager.

He dipped his tongue between her lips, tasting more of her and never getting enough. His mouth wanted her, his hands and his cock wanted her. Fingers moved up her ribcage, pulling the scrap of Lycra over one tit so he could tease her nipple. She moaned into his mouth, which only made him want to pleasure her more just to hear his name in her sexy voice.

Moving away from her lips, he bent his head down to her luscious breasts. Perfect; not too big and not too small with light pink nipples. He took one into his mouth, and she cried his name and dug her fingers into his hair.

Her scent was driving him crazy, and he wanted more of it. He moved his hand down, over her flat stomach and lower still, waiting for her protests. When he heard none, he delved under her bikini bottom. Christ, she was soaking wet. Her pussy lips were slick with her juices, and it was easy to slip a finger inside her.

She bucked her hips up, meeting his finger eagerly. When he drew her nipple harder into his mouth, her body shuddered and he heard her let out a muffled moan. Her honey scent exploded around him, and it was like everything else disappeared and his entire world only consisted of Violet.

The rise and fall of her chest slowed down, and he looked up at her. Violet's eyes were closed, but her plump lips were parted. He withdrew his hand from her bottoms and put it up to his mouth, licking it clean. Fuck, she was delicious, and he wanted to have more of her. But that could wait. He had to have her now.

Nathan moved above her, covering her body with his. She looked up at him and blinked, her pupils still blown out with desire. He lowered his head again and she kissed him back eagerly, her hands moving down to his shorts to pull them low over his hips.

"Wow. Classy you two. Just classy," came Kate's droll voice, followed by a short gasp.

Nathan cursed and rolled off the car, taking Violet with him. They got to their feet, and he pulled up his shorts as Violet straightened herself out. "What the fuck, Kate? What are you guys doing here?"

"Excuse me," she said. "This is a family event. And," she pointed to Sybil, who was standing next to her with her hands over her eyes, "you've scarred poor Sybil for life."

"Shut up, Kate!" Sybil put her hands down. "I'm sorry! We saw you take her away, and I thought—"

"You thought what?" Nathan asked.

"You were angry, and then you dragged her off like a caveman!" Sybil exclaimed. "What were we supposed to think?"

"I think Violet was enjoying herself in the cave just fine," Kate said with a raised brow.

Nathan sent his sister a death glare. "Just get out, will you?"

"All right, all right. But let me remind you again this is a *family* affair, and there are shifter kids with sensitive hearing everywhere. Matthew and Jason'll have your head if they even hear of anything inappropriate," Sybil warned.

"So go get a room you horn dogs!" Kate added. With a wave of her hand, she turned and disappeared back into the woods, taking Sybil with her.

"I'm sorry," Violet began. "I—"

"You're *sorry?*" he asked. "Sorry?"

She bit her lip. "I was the one who … who …"

"Kissed me?" he said with a smirk.

That cold mask slipped over her face. "Yes. So all of this was my fault."

"It's no one's fault."

She picked up the discarded towel and wrapped it around herself. "Look, we both agreed we don't want to be mates. And that's fine."

"Just wait a minute! I never said that," he protested. "Violet—"

"Really, Nathan." She sighed. "Don't think just because we … did what we did that you have to spare my feelings. I'm not some inexperienced virgin or one of your conquests that you have to give the gentle let-down to the next morning. I happen to be a grown woman."

She stood there like nothing happened between them. Like it wasn't just moments ago he was kissing her and touching her before she came apart in his arms. *Cold-hearted and calculated.* He swallowed the lump in his throat. "Fine. I'll see you on Monday."

"Nathan? Are you angry at—"

"I said it's fine."

He opened the door to his Mustang, and grabbed the keys from the hidden compartment under the seat. Slipping the key into the ignition, he turned the engine and put the gear in reverse, gunning it out of there and leaving Violet standing in the clearing by herself. He knew it was immature, but he didn't know what else to do. His wolf was howling in anger and pain, and he didn't want to feel that anymore.

CHAPTER SIX

Violet watched as the car backed up and disappeared down the winding wooded path. When she thought she was alone, she finally allowed her knees to buckle.

"No," she said aloud, holding onto the nearest thing she could grab. No, she couldn't give into Nathan.

But she already did. No, that was wrong. She didn't give into Nathan; she was the one who pulled him into that kiss. And let him push her back onto the hood of his car. And spread her legs and let him touch her until she—

Mine, her tiger moaned in an unhappy voice.

"We have to stay focused. Remember why we can't stay here."

Violet pulled the towel closer around her and decided to make her way back to the picnic. Oh dear, it had been embarrassing, getting caught like that by Kate and Sybil. And of course, probably everyone saw Nathan carrying her away. That cad.

But, as she walked through the thick thicket of trees, she

couldn't help but remember the feel of his lips on hers and his tongue on her nipples. The way his fingers touched her and made her orgasm …

And then he left, angry at her. But why was he mad? An unfamiliar, uncomfortable feeling crept into her chest.

Mine!

"Shut up, you horny kitty! This wouldn't have happened if you could control yourself! You should—" She gasped. *That's it.*

As a scientist, Violet was taught to find solutions to problems. And her professors always said that sometimes unconventional methods were necessary. She may have just found a way to solve her problem, both with her tiger and Nathan.

Come Monday morning, Violet had fully convinced herself that she had found the solution. Now, all she had to do was convince Nathan it would be the right thing to do.

She came to work prepared with what she was going to say. He wasn't in their shared office, so she went ahead and finished her tasks, gathering samples and checking on potential future veins to mine. By the time she returned to the trailer, Nathan was sitting at his desk, his face drawn into a frown as he stared at his computer screen. When he saw her, his scowl deepened and the room seemed to grow colder. It only convinced her she was doing the right thing.

"Oh good, you're here." She dropped the bag of samples on her desk and then walked to his side of the office.

He let out a grunt and looked back at his screen.

"Nathan," she began. No reaction from him.

"Nathan," she repeated. He continued to ignore her. She let

out a sigh and walked closer to him, walking around his desk so she could stand over him. "Are you just going to ignore me?"

He remained still for a few seconds then looked up at her, his eyes glinting like hard emeralds. "What do you want?"

"Look, I'm sorry about what happened on Saturday."

"You've already said you're sorry."

But you haven't said you forgive me. That thought came out of nowhere. She brushed it aside. "Right. And I mean it. But, I think it's best if we clear the air. I can't keep working in an environment where we're both angry or distracted. So, I've come up with a solution."

His expression changed from indifference to curiosity. "You have, have you?"

"Yes." She took a deep breath. "The sexual attraction between us is obvious. Perhaps it's a function of our biologies as shifters. Our animals obviously think we'd be highly compatible partners."

"Uh … " He looked confused now.

Violet bit her lip. She tended to go on different tangents, so she supposed the more direct approach would work better. "I propose we consummate our relationship in order to satisfy our animal urges and perhaps create a more genial and even productive working environment."

"Excuse me?"

Oh dear, did this man really possess a degree? Did he not understand the words she was saying? Should she make them simpler? "What I'm trying to say is we should have sexual intercourse to relieve the tension between us." There, she said it. It was the perfect solution to their problem. He obviously wanted her, and she thought his performance the other day was more than adequate. Okay, a lot adequate.

Much more adequate than anyone she'd ever been with before.

His eyes seemed to glass over but when they cleared, she saw a flash of ... something in there. He muttered a curse and stood up. "I thought that's what you meant." He grabbed her shoulders and flipped their positions, so she was trapped between him and his desk.

"So you agree?" she asked.

"To have sex with you?"

She shivered involuntarily when he touched her cheek with a finger. "Yes." He leaned in close. Oh, was he going to kiss her now? "I'm free tonight, if your schedule is open."

"I'll have to check with my secretary," he bit out. "So, you want to share your hot little body with me—"

"We would be 'sharing' each other," she corrected. And oh ... he was so close she could feel the warmth of his body against her. She wanted to feel the hard muscles of his chest under her palms again.

"And then after?"

She blinked. After? Did he mean he wanted more than one night? "I think once should be enough, don't you agree? What more could you possibly want? Besides, I won't be staying in this little town forever." Blackstone was quaint, but she was needed elsewhere.

The tension in the air broke.

"No thanks," he said, shoving away from her. "I don't want *anything* from you."

Violet felt like she was doused with a bucket of ice water.

A ringing sound from the desk made Violet jump away. Nathan grabbed the receiver forcefully and answered the line. He said a few brief words and put it down. "Well, I gotta go. See ya around."

"Oh." That cold feeling seeped into her bones, into her very core. He was angry at her. Again.

She put her up hands in frustration. "Men," she muttered as she sat back at her desk.

This is why she didn't have long-term relationships. Her parents always said sex was natural and encouraged her to explore her sexuality. Many of her previous partners were only happy to be in a casual relationship with her; she usually picked men who had their own goals and were simply too busy to be tied down like her. She thought Nathan would be the same, but clearly she read him wrong.

Mine, the tiger whined.

A flash of memory from Saturday surfaced in her brain. Did he fake that? But then again, she kissed him. Perhaps he didn't want her to be embarrassed, so he kept going with the charade.

"Ugh." No, this was it. Done and over. She would just have to get through the next few weeks and hope her funding would come through soon and she could leave this place.

She spent the rest of the day keeping herself busy. It was a good thing she had learned to compartmentalize her emotions, locking them away so she could perform her duties. Even though her heart wasn't in it, she still had a job to do and she couldn't disappoint Dr. Philipps by slacking off just because she was feeling miffed. Nathan never did come back to the office, which suited her just fine. However, she was surprised by the person who walked into the trailer right before she was going to clock out.

"Ben," she greeted the bear shifter as stood in the doorway.

"Violet. May I come in?"

"Of course. I'm actually on my way out, though. But I can wait."

Ben sat down on the chair in front of her desk. "I won't keep you. I just need a couple of minutes."

"Was my work for the day not satisfactory?" she asked, her brows drawing together. "I know it took me a while to collect those samples, but I wanted to make sure I did them right and—"

He put a hand up. "Oh no, not at all. You're doing a fine job. It's not that. Er," he rubbed the back of his head. "It's about Nathan."

"What about Nathan?"

"Well … I was wondering, uh …" He shifted uncomfortably. "He seemed really … upset today. He just left without saying goodbye."

"Upset?" He barely showed any emotion when he left. He was downright cold.

"Yeah. I was wondering if you said something to upset him. Not that I blame you or anything. Oh shit." He stood up. "Sorry, this is probably a personal matter. Between you two. I was concerned as a friend, but maybe I shouldn't be asking you this."

Irritation pricked at her. "Why would *he* be upset? I offered him sexual intercourse, and he was the one who turned me down."

Ben's jaw dropped. "Right. This really is inappropriate, so I'll be going now."

"Wait!" Perhaps Ben could help shed some light on this mystery. "Ben, wait. I'd like to talk to you. As Nathan's friend and not my boss."

"Oh. Uhm, I'm not really comfortable—"

"How long have you known him?"

"Er, pretty much since we were kids."

"So you know him well?"

He scratched his chin. "I guess you could say that."

"Last Saturday we almost had intercourse in his car. I mean, not in his car, but *on* his car."

"Violet—"

"We were interrupted, which is why I had to qualify the event as 'almost.' But then I realized we were both attracted to each other, unattached, and obviously sexually compatible. It made sense."

"As your boss, I don't think you should be saying the s-word around me."

Violet continued. "So, when I offered him a no-strings attached sex—, uh, arrangement, he turned me down."

"Uhm, don't you have female friends you can talk to about this?" Ben asked.

She stood up and slammed her palms on the table. "Please, Ben, I'm trying to figure him out. What did I say that upset him?"

Ben sighed and leaned back in his chair. "You want to know the honest truth, Violet?"

She sat back down. "Please enlighten me."

"I've known Nathan since we were kids, though I was a grade ahead in school. A year after I went to Colorado State to study mining engineering, he followed me to complete the same degree. Double major, along with advanced math. Most people think he's some dumb jock because he's kind of a party animal and has a reputation with the ladies. But he did well in school, even graduated summa cum laude."

"I never would have guessed."

"Well, yeah, people tend to underestimate him a lot. He likes to put on a show, see? But I think, well … he's much more sensitive than that."

"Oh." A feeling of dread crept into her.

"Maybe, just maybe, when you offered se—*that* to him, he might have been insulted."

It all clicked into place. Violet cursed her bluntness. Not everything was about science and logic. She kept forgetting people weren't like machines or experiments. While she thought she was being logical and smart about the whole thing, she had inadvertently been cold and clinical. She basically treated him like a piece of meat without any regard for his feelings whatsoever.

"Huh." She made up her mind. "I need to speak with Nathan. And to apologize. For real this time. Where might I find him after hours? Do you have his address?"

"Uh, well. I imagine he'd be at The Den. It's a local bar here."

"Right. I could look it up."

"I'm actually headed there myself later in the evening," Ben said. "Penny's a waitress there and her shift starts at seven. But we're meeting for dinner. You're welcome to join us."

"Oh, I couldn't intrude." She supposed a bar would be more of a neutral territory and better than showing up at his house unannounced. "If you give me the address, I could show up when he's there."

"I can't guarantee he'll be there."

"It's fine." She had to see him, and she wasn't sure she could wait until tomorrow. If Nathan could find ways to avoid her at work, she might never see him again. "I'll take my chances."

CHAPTER SEVEN

NATHAN HUNCHED over the bar as the bartender, Heather, placed his beer in front of him. He gave her a grateful nod and stared at the pale gold liquid but didn't move to touch it. Alcohol wouldn't do anything for him right now anyway.

He considered staying home after work and not talking to anyone, but he already did that for most of the weekend. After what happened at the picnic, he didn't want to be around people. He drove deeper into the mountains, and once he thought he was far enough away, shifted into his wolf form and let it roam as much as it wanted. It was begging him to be free, and after the whole debacle with Violet, he was only happy to give in. He woke up the next day and made his way back to his car. He thought letting his wolf free would make him feel much better, but he was only more confused. Monday morning came far too early. He was still unsure of what to say to Violet, so he went in to work late hoping to avoid her.

Then, she saunters up to him, tells him she's *sorry* she

kissed him, and proposes they sleep together to relieve the sexual tension between them. *So they could work better.*

Sure, he'd had numerous one-night stands in the past, but he liked to think he treated the girls he slept with with respect. He was straight with them, never promising more but always making sure they left satisfied and happy. No, he didn't treat it like some business arrangement or scientific experiment. It only solidified the fact that Violet was cold and calculated with no feelings whatsoever.

A muscle flicked angrily in his jaw. He decided right then and there he was done. Done with Violet Robichaux. He hoped she would leave Blackstone soon, so he would never have to see her again.

Mine.

"Shut the fuck up!" Nathan slammed his fist down so hard his glass shook, splashing beer all over the bar top. Heather gave him a disapproving look, and he shot her a sheepish smile as he reached over the counter for a dry rag to mop up the mess.

"Nathan?"

He whipped around at the sound of the voice. "Melanie?" He didn't recognize her at first. The night they met, she'd been all dolled up. Now, her face was make-up free, her hair was piled on top of her head in a messy bun, and she was wearing sweats.

"Nathan," she cried in relief. "I'm so glad you're here. I was waiting for you last night but you didn't come."

"Melanie, what's wrong?" He noticed the deep bags under her eyes. "Are you okay?"

She took a hard gulp, then tears began to roll down her cheeks. "I didn't know what else to do or who to turn to."

"Melanie—" He nearly jumped when she threw herself in

his arms and pressed her face into his chest. Gingerly, he rubbed a hand down her back. "It's okay," he soothed. "Tell me what's wrong."

"It's my sister … Joanne. She's missing. I went to her apartment on Friday, but she wasn't there. None of her friends have seen her for two days, and she's missed all of her classes. I've been calling her, but her phone keeps going to voice mail and I've already left a hundred messages."

"Did you call the police?"

She nodded. "I went to Verona Mills P.D. and they asked me a few questions, but they think she just ran away. They said they'd keep an eye out, but they refuse to do anything else until she's been missing for a few days."

"Maybe she needed a break?"

"No," she protested. "Joanne would never run away like that! She tells me everything and as far as I know, there was nothing wrong. She loved her classes, her professors, and she doesn't drink or party."

"What do you think happened?"

"I went to her apartment. I didn't find anything." She gave a small laugh. "It was clean. Much more than it usually is. Like someone had cleaned it. All her clothes were there."

He gently pried her arms away from him. "So, why come to me?"

"You said you owed me a favor, right?"

"Sure."

"Flight shifters have great eyesight from a distance, but our sense of smell is pretty much shit. I want you to come with me and see if you can sniff out any clues. I think someone may have taken her."

"You want me to go to your sister's apartment and smell her stuff?"

She let out a long sigh. "I know. It's a long shot, but I'm desperate. I can't wait on the police. What if something happened to her? And you know humans don't really care about our kind." Her gaze dropped to the ground. "The moment they found out she was a shifter, it was like they lost interest."

Nathan's hands clenched into fists. He'd been living in the Blackstone bubble so long he'd forgotten how cruel humans were to shifters. In fact, his own parents had faced the same prejudice themselves. They were run out of their small town in the middle of the night because someone outed them as wolf shifters. If they hadn't thought of leaving and heading to Blackstone, who knows what would have happened and how his life would have turned out. "All right. Let's go have a sniff before any scents disappear."

Her eyes went wide. "Really?"

"Yeah, of course."

"Oh Nathan, thank you!" She launched herself into his arms and hugged him tight.

"I haven't done anything yet," he said. "We should—" A strange sensation prickled down the back of his neck, and his wolf stood at attention. As he looked up, his gaze crashed into familiar light blue eyes.

Violet stood right behind Melanie, her posture stiff and her face expressionless. For a brief moment, he thought he saw something flash in her eyes. Slowly, he let Melanie go and marched toward Violet.

Complete and utter shock was coursing through his system, and he said the first thing that came to mind. "What are you doing here?"

"Nothing," she said in a flat tone. "Absolutely nothing." She quickly pivoted and began to walk out of the room.

"Fuck!" He didn't know why he gave a damn. Violet could think whatever she wanted to think, and he didn't owe her any explanation. But it was like his feet had a life of their own, and he found himself going after her.

He caught her arm as she reached the door. "Violet!"

"Let go," she said, yanking her arm away.

"I can explain."

"You don't have to explain anything." Her face was calm, but he could feel her animal's anger. It was practically hissing and spitting at him. His own wolf was furious at him for riling up their mate. Her gaze traveled behind him. "I see you're busy. I shouldn't have bothered you."

"It's not what you think."

"This is exactly what I think. But don't worry, I can take a hint. You said it yourself that day at the mines. You don't want me."

"Why do you keep saying that?" He tried to grasp her again, but she evaded him. "I never said that to you!"

Her eyes blazed. "Newsflash Ben: I don't want her either."

Blood drained from his face. "You heard that?"

"Does it matter? Anyway, I won't be bothering you again."

She didn't even look back; instead she pushed against the doors, disappearing from his sight. And he stood there, staring dumbly. He did say those words, but only because he wanted to get Ben off his back. *Damn I'm an idiot.*

He went after her, but when he reached the parking lot, she was gone. Sniffing the air, he picked up her scent and followed his nose until he found her in the rear part of the building, struggling with her car door.

"Damn thing," she cursed. "I'm bringing you back to the rental place tomorrow, you piece of—"

"Violet," he called. He was next to her in an instant.

She started, and before she could jump away, her grabbed her arms and held her in place. "Stop!"

"No, you stop!" She wiggled, but he didn't let her go. "Why are you—"

"Nathan, what's going on?"

Shit. He had forgotten all about Melanie.

Violet stopped struggling. "Your *date* is waiting."

Melanie gasped. "Date? Oh no. Crap, I knew I had gotten you into trouble." She walked closer to them. "I'm sorry you got the wrong impression. We weren't here to hook up or anything."

"You're not?"

"He's already turned me down." She gave Nathan a knowing glance.

"Turned you down?" Violet asked.

"Yeah, long story," Nathan said.

Melanie continued. "I came here because I need Nathan's help. He owes me a favor." She took something from her pocket and put it in front of Violet's face. "He's going to help me find her." She quickly explained about her sister, repeating what she had told Nathan. Much to his surprise, Violet relaxed although she did tense up when Melanie finished her story.

"So, you have no idea where your sister is?"

Melanie shook her head. "I swear, I've tried everything. Something's happened to her, I know it."

Violet placed her hands on Melanie's shoulders. "We'll help you."

"Hold on," Nathan began. "What do you mean *we*?"

"I mean you and me. My sense of smell isn't as good as yours, but I can still pick up trace scents," she said. "We can cover more ground quickly. Does your sister have a vehicle?"

"Yes," Melanie said, her face lighting up. "It was still in her parking space."

"All right. We can search her apartment and her car. Do you know of any other places she frequents?"

"I can think of a few," Melanie said. "But … you don't have to do this, uh …"

"Violet," she said. "I'm Violet."

"Melanie."

"Right. Melanie, if your sister is missing and the authorities refuse to help, then we have no choice but to assist you. Right, Nathan?"

"Yes, but—"

"I'm here and I can help, so of course I will. Now," she straightened her shoulders, "I'll ride with Nathan and we'll follow you in your car. We should go now. Scents and other clues may be degrading as we speak, especially in this weather."

Nathan shrugged. "My car's out front." This wasn't working out the way he thought it would, but he'd take it.

where they could sleep in exchange for extra supplies and money.

Unfortunately the village was also very backward, and because she was an unmarried woman, no one would let her stay on their property. Some old wives' tale. It was bad luck, they said. She offered them double what was in the agreement, but it didn't persuade them. She was frustrated and had nearly lost hope when an older woman approached her as she was walking by herself figuring out what to do.

Her name was Antonia, she had said. She ran the local girl's orphanage just outside of town. Antonia took on the girls no one wanted, the girls who had no parents because they lost their lives to the war or the ones who were in danger of being exploited.

So it seemed Antonia would be taking on another unwanted female. She followed Antonia a good thirty-minute walk from the main village to the dusty, run-down brick home where she ran her orphanage.

It was perfect. Actually, she didn't care; all she needed was a place to put up her tent as she would spend most of her time exploring the mountains with her team anyway. When she arrived, twenty-three girls, the youngest around two years old and the oldest nearly fourteen, were waiting for them. They greeted Antonia warmly but Violet with wary and curious eyes. She shrugged. She had no use for children. To her they took up too much time and resources and detracted away from more important things, like research and learning.

Every morning at seven a.m. she would leave the orphanage to head out to the village and come back after dark. The girls watched her but never approached. When her first day off came around, she was relaxing under tree, eating a protein bar and reading a book, when she felt someone's presence nearby.

Clear green eyes peered up at her. The little girl blinked and when Violet smiled at her, her face broke into a gap-toothed grin. That was the first time she met Nadia.

It was strange how her face was so vivid in her mind even though it was nearly six months ago when she first saw the girl. Her face was small but clean, and she had the whitest blonde hair Violet had ever seen.

Her heart began to pound as she recalled a different, even more vivid, memory. Red. Blood red everywhere. On her paws and on her fur. On soft white blonde hair and lifeless limbs.

"We're here."

Nathan's voice jarred Violet out of her memories.

"Violet, are you okay?"

She didn't even realize her heart was pounding in her chest or that she had been wringing her hands together until her knuckles turned pale. "I'm fine." Yanking the door handle, she stepped out.

Melanie had parked her car right beside Nathan's, and she was already waiting for them outside of the four-story brick building. She waved them over.

"I have a spare set of keys," she explained as they entered the apartment building. They walked all the way up to the third floor and stopped at the first door on the left.

"Wait," Violet said. "You should go inside and grab us something of Joanne's—something only she would touch, if possible."

"Why?" Melanie asked.

"To establish a base scent," Nathan answered. "We need to

know what she smells like, so we can distinguish anything inside that's not her or you."

"Gotcha." Melanie scratched at her chin. "I think I know what would work." She disappeared into the apartment and came back after a few moments. She held out a faded pink piece of fabric. "She always sleeps with this. It was her baby blanket." Her face drew into a worried expression. "Now, I'm even more sure she didn't just run away on her own. She would never leave without this."

Nathan took the blanket and gave it a sniff before handing it to Violet. "Okay, let's go inside."

Melanie led them into the apartment. It was small but clean and looked lived in. They were standing in the living room which had a couch, a coffee table, and TV. On the left, Violet could see a doorway that led into a kitchen. A door on the right side was most likely the bedroom.

"I'll take this room since it's the biggest," Nathan said.

"I'll go into the bedroom," Violet volunteered.

As she guessed, the door on the right did lead her into the small bedroom. A double bed was squeezed up against the corner, and next to it was a bedside table with a lamp. She walked there first and sat on the mattress. It was made and smelled clean. Leaning down on the pillow, she could pick up Joanne's scent—feathers and something citrusy. As far as she could tell, no one else had been in here recently.

As she turned her head, the framed photo on the bedside table caught her eye. It was a picture of two little girls, one older and one younger, obviously related. *Joanne and Melanie.*

It was Joanne's picture that had unlocked those memories of Nadia. Her hair wasn't as light, but the innocent smile reminded her of the little girl. And that's when she knew she had to help find Joanne. To atone for her failure.

"Violet!" came Melanie's voice from the living room. "Come quick!"

Violet got to her feet. "What is it?" she asked as she joined the others.

The couch that had been in the middle of the room was pushed aside and Nathan was on his knees, his nose pressed to the hardwood floor. His brows were knitted together in concentration. "Shit," he cursed.

"What is it?" Melanie asked in a tentative voice.

Nathan pushed himself up. "Blood. Lots of it. Probably a couple of days old."

"Oh no." Melanie's voice broke and tears pooled at her eyes. "Joanne."

Violet put an arm around her. "There, there. You and Joanne are shifters, right?"

Melanie nodded. "We're owls."

"She might have been struck on the head. Such wounds can cause a lot of blood loss," Violet began. "The injury she took most likely broke the skin on her skull and there are so many blood vessels in there. In fact, twenty percent of the blood your heart pumps goes up to the brain and—"

"Violet," Nathan said in a warning voice.

Melanie looked even paler and not comforted by her words at all. "Oh, sorry. Anyway, my point is, since Joanne is a shifter, it's likely she's already healed."

"Oh." Melanie seemed a little more relieved.

Violet walked over to the where Nathan was kneeling. "So, you think someone cleaned it?"

"Definitely."

Melanie's eyes lit up. "There was a carpet there. I'm pretty sure."

"When she bled out, they could have gotten rid of the

carpet and mopped up what was left," Violet said. "As long as they made it look like she ran away, it could be days before the police sent over any forensic experts."

"If they send one at all," Nathan added, his jaw set.

"Anything else you can pick up?" Melanie asked.

"Let me try," Violet said. "My nose is a little more fresh." She knelt down beside Nathan and lowered her head to the floor. "Hmm … I don't smell—" Her body went still.

"Violet?"

"Did you scent something?" Nathan asked.

"No, but …" She crawled over to the couch. There was something stuck under one of the feet. Lifting the couch, she picked it up. It was hair. Specifically a bunch of long dark hair with a piece of a bloody scalp stuck to one end.

"What's that—eww, gross!" Melanie recoiled.

Violet held it up to her nose. There were trace amounts of Joanne's scent and someone else—the owner of the hair, of course.

"Motherfucker," Nathan cursed. He grabbed the hair from Violet and sniffed it. "Melanie, can you get a bag for this?" Melanie nodded and ran to the kitchen. "Did you find anything else down there?"

Violet peered under the couch. "Nothing, I'm afraid."

"Nathan! Violet!"

They looked at each other. Nathan helped her up, and they headed to the kitchen.

"What's wrong?" Nathan asked.

"This!" Melanie held up a small piece of cardboard.

"Huh?" Nathan took it from her fingers. "It's a matchbook."

"Yes, but look! It's for that seedy biker bar just outside of town. The Bitter End. I found it on the floor under the kitchen table."

Nathan shrugged. "So?"

"I told you!" Melanie exclaimed. "Joanne never goes to bars. And even if she did, it wouldn't be there. It's where the Kings of Death hang out."

"Kings of Death?" Violet echoed.

"Yeah, they're a notorious biker gang," Nathan said. "They keep out of Blackstone, but their exploits are known in the area. Gunrunning, drugs, armed robbery, to name a few."

"See? Joanne would never go to such a place. Whoever took her must have dropped this accidentally."

"It seems sloppy," Nathan said.

"But plausible," Violet added. She took the matchbook from Melanie and sniffed it. "Scent's not the same as the hair, but it's not Joanne's either. Could be a second accomplice. We should go to The Bitter End and check it out."

"Check it out?" Nathan asked in an incredulous voice. "Are you insane?"

"We can't waste any more time," Violet said. She would not make the same mistake twice.

"No," Nathan said. "We are not going to that biker bar. We're going to go to the police and—"

"The police won't help us," cried Melanie. "They don't care about her."

Nathan crossed his arms over his chest. "I'm not taking you there."

Violet stood toe-to-toe with him. "We don't need your help or your permission. Melanie and I can go by ourselves."

"No fucking way," he said. But the two women stood their ground. He let out a frustrated groan and took his keys from his pocket. "Fine. We're going, but you two are going to stay in the car while I go in there and gather info." He grabbed the matchbook from Violet. "Let's go."

CHAPTER NINE

NATHAN KNEW this was a bad idea the moment he walked into The Bitter End and several pair of eyes zeroed in on him. The name of the bar seemed poetic at the moment.

He told himself over and over again it was a bad idea. He should have said fuck it and gunned it to the police station where they could turn over their evidence to the authorities. That was the right thing to do. But, somehow, he knew Melanie was right. The police didn't care enough to take Joanne's disappearance seriously in the first place. This evidence might change their mind, but no way were they going to investigate fast enough. Joanne could be in real danger. And Violet's determination only made him want to find her more.

But walking into a biker bar by himself? That was probably a stupid move. He wasn't going to let the girls in here, though.

He motioned for the bartender, a sour-faced man with a large potbelly that stuck out of his leather vest, to bring him another beer. It was his second. He had nursed his first, hoping to keep a low profile and scope out the place. Not that it did any good. He looked down at his flannel work shirt and clean jeans. He looked like a Goddamn Eagle Scout next to the lowlifes around him.

The bartender came closer and placed a bottle in front of him. "You're not from around here, are you?"

No shit, Sherlock. He bit his tongue but knew this was his chance. Bartenders always knew everything that went on in his or her establishment. This would be his in, a way for him to see if the Kings of Death—

A crash from behind had him wincing. "What the—Motherfucker!" He shot to his feet when he saw what had caused the commotion. Or rather *who.* After tossing a couple of bills on the bar, he strode angrily across the room.

The man who was backed up against the wall was six feet tall and probably two hundred pounds of pure muscle. He was wearing a black leather vest and matching pants, and his arms were covered in tattoos. Around him were broken pieces of furniture, obviously destroyed as he crashed into them. The biker should have looked fierce, but Nathan saw real fear in the man's eyes as Violet walked up to him and grabbed him by the throat.

"I said tell me where she is," she said in a deadly calm voice.

"Violet," Nathan said. "Baby, you gotta let him go."

Her eyes blazed with pure fury. "It's him. I can *smell* him." Her hand squeezed tighter, and the man's face began to turn blue.

He leaned in closer. "Fuck." She was right. That was the scent on the hair. He reached out to push the man's head to the side. Right on the backside of his head was a healing wound where a chunk of scalp had been pulled out.

"Violet, he's about to pass out," he said. "Just … give him a little air so we can talk to him, yeah?"

She loosened her grip, and the man's face returned to normal. "Where is she?" Violet said. "Where's Joanne? Where did your gang stash her?"

The man gurgled out an answer that sounded negative, but that only made Violet seem angrier.

"What's going on here?"

Oh fuck.

Nathan turned around. Nearly a dozen guys in matching leather vests surrounded them, their expressions fierce. One of them stepped forward. Every inch of exposed skin was covered in tattoos, including his shaved head, and a patch over the right side of his vest read "President."

"Tell me what's going on. I'm not gonna ask again," he began.

"Look, we don't want to cause trouble—"

"*You're* not, but *she* came in here lookin' for it." He walked over to Violet, then looked at Nathan. "This your woman?"

Her light eyes glowed. "I most certainly do not belong to anyone, and you may address me directly."

The president's eyes narrowed. "You one of those shifters from that town?"

"We are," she said. For a brief moment, Violet's eyes turned to slits. That would have scared a lesser man, but the president didn't even flinch.

"Look, we don't go into your town, so I was hoping you'd do us the courtesy of not encroaching in our territory," he said. "What's your beef with Ruiz? Did he crash your knitting club or somethin'?" His men jeered and chuckled.

Nathan raised both his hands. "Like I said, we don't want any trouble—"

"He kidnapped my friend's sister," Violet interrupted. "We have proof. Now, tell us where you're hiding her or we'll go to the police."

The president laughed, then turned back to his men. "This chick sure is crazy," he cackled and the other men began to laugh as well.

"We know you have her," Violet said. "Where is she?" She gripped Ruiz's throat tighter, making the man choke again.

The president held his hand up and the room went silent. "Listen here, girly. First of all, I don't know what you're talking about. We do a lot of things that aren't exactly legal, but kidnapping innocent girls ain't one of them. In fact, I've made it a rule in my club that hurting women and children is the one line we won't cross. Now," he looked at Ruiz, "if what you say is true, then he's broken our biggest rule, which means he answers to *us*."

"It is true," Nathan said. "Like she said, we have proof."

"What proof?"

Nathan took out the plastic bag from his pocket. "Here. This is your guy's hair, pulled right from his scalp. We found it in the living room of our missing friend. She's a shifter too, and she's strong enough to do that kind of damage."

"Yeah? What if they were just having a bit of rough fun and she got a little too excited?"

"Prez," one of the guys from behind stepped forward. "Ruiz told us his hair got caught in the brake rod of his hog while he was fixin' it."

"Yeah," someone else added. "You know if some chick he was bangin' did that, he woulda made sure we all knew."

Nathan saw a flicker of doubt in the president's face. He

took out the matchbook. "We found this in her kitchen, kicked under the table. This is how we got here. You know about us shifters, right? We can smell real good and someone else left a clue."

"So?"

"We picked up another scent from this." Nathan nodded to the rest of the men. "So, you might have a second rule-breaker in your gang."

The president's eyes turned cold. "All right then. Show me what you got."

Nathan walked toward the group of men. Thank God his nose was sensitive enough so he didn't have to get too close. Cautiously, he approached the first one, a tall skinny guy with thinning hair and took a sniff. *No.* The white-haired man next to him was another negative. As neared the third one, a young man with spiked hair, alarm bells went off in his head and he smelled the same trace scent from the matchbook. He looked the kid straight in the eye. "You got anything to say?"

The young man's eyes widened in surprise, and Nathan could smell the fear coming off him. "N-n-no!"

"You sure?"

"I—" He shoved at Nathan and then tried to get past him. But, with his quick reflexes, Nathan grabbed the kid by his vest collar and slammed him on the ground.

"Motherfucker! Ellis!" The president knelt down and picked him up. "You son of a bitch!" He looked back at Ruiz. "You two been moonlightin' on me?"

Violet let go of Ruiz, and he collapsed to his knees. "Asshole rat," he choked at Ellis, his meaty hands rubbing at his throat.

"I-I-I'm sorry, Prez," Ellis cried. "I was just … he said it was easy money. Those girls ... we didn't hurt them or nothing. Just delivered them."

"Girls?" Violet's voice had the fury of an avenging angel. "There were more?"

"J-j-just one more," Ellis said. "He said no one was gonna find out. Not even you, Prez."

"Take these pieces of shit away," Prez said. Four men came forward and dragged Ellis and Ruiz away and disappeared into a door in the back of the bar.

"Hey!" Violet said in an indignant tone. "What about my friend? We need to question your men! Bring them back and—"

Prez laughed in her face. "Question them? Sure, if there's anything left of them by the time we're done."

"But you can't—"

"Let's go." Nathan grabbed Violet by the elbow. He could see Prez growing agitated. He could probably take two or three of the men at a time, but if they were packing heat, which they probably were, that could slow him down even in wolf form.

"But—"

"Violet, let's go!" He grabbed her by the waist and pulled her across the room, ignoring her protests. When they were outside of The Bitter End, she pulled away from him.

"How could you just let them get away?" Violet accused. "We still have to talk to them!"

"Violet, there was no way those men were going to let us interrogate their members. These clubs have strict codes of conduct, and they deal with problems internally."

"Are they going to kill those two men?"

"I don't think so," Nathan said. "They broke a rule, so I'm

sure they'll be punished or expelled. But we need to get help if we want to find Joanne and any other girls."

Violet seemed to calm down. "Are we going to the police?"

Nathan shook his head. "No, they won't be any help. But I know someone who can help us."

They explained what happened to Melanie, who had been waiting in her car in the parking lot.

"What do we do now?" she asked, her lower lip trembling.

"We're gonna head back to Blackstone and talk to the Lennoxes. They can help."

"We'll find her," Violet said.

"Keep me informed and please call me for anything," Melanie said. "I'll be taking a few days off from work to hand out flyers. I also … need to tell my mom."

"Good luck," Nathan said. "We'll call you if anything comes up."

As soon as Melanie's car was gone, Nathan and Violet walked back to his car.

"I know the Lennoxes consider themselves the protectors of the shifters of Blackstone," Violet said as they drove back. "But why would Matthew or Jason Lennox bother themselves with one missing shifter?"

Nathan looked straight ahead at the dark highway. "We're not going to ask for help from Matthew or Jason."

"Then who?"

"I can't tell you yet. But trust me."

The ride back was silent, and Nathan was glad Violet didn't ask him anymore questions. It would be difficult enough to explain what they were doing, let alone tell Violet about how he was going to help find Joanne.

He drove to the newer development on the south side of Blackstone. The town had expanded a lot over the years, but the Main Street area was preserved because of its quaint small-town charm that tourists loved. The Lennox Corporation developed South Blackstone as a trendy and hip neighborhood to attract younger people to come and work and live in the town. He pulled into the group of low-rise loft buildings and eased his car into an empty parking spot.

Nathan led Violet into the first building, pressing the button for the top floor. Each floor only had one apartment, so he rang the bell of the lone door outside the elevator.

"Nathan? Dr. Robichaux?" Jason Lennox stood in the doorway, a perplexed look on his face. "What are you guys doing here?"

"Where's Christina?"

"She's kinda busy right now," Jason said. "What's this about?"

"We need her help. Specifically, The Agency's help."

Jason's gaze flickered at Violet. "You know you can't just say that out loud, man."

"This is an emergency."

His friend let out a sigh. "Well, we actually were going to sit down and work on a few things. There's someone else here, too."

Jason opened the door to reveal his adopted brother, Luke Lennox, sitting on the couch. "Luke?" Nathan said.

Luke nodded his head at him. "Nathan." His gaze landed briefly on Violet, but he didn't say anything.

"Come on in," Jason said. Nathan entered first, followed by

Violet. "Luke, this is Dr. Violet Robichaux. She's replacing Dr. Philipps at the mines."

"Temporarily," Violet added. "How do you do?"

Luke raised a blond brow at her. "Temporarily?"

"It's a long story," she sighed, then turned to Nathan. "I still don't understand what we're doing here."

"Jason," Nathan began. "We really have to talk to Christina."

"She's in her office on a conference call with her father. He's in Fiji. Or Indonesia, I forget. Anyway, we were going to discuss, uh, *business* with Luke. He's eager to get on with his night, so why don't we go in and interrupt her?"

The four of them walked down the hallway off the living room of the loft. Jason opened the last door on the right and ushered them inside.

"Really, Papa?" Christina Lennox sat behind the desk, staring at a computer screen. She was wearing a headset and when she saw them walk in, she waved them to come over. "All right then. If you're sure he's the one you want to send. You really can't spare Angel? Fine. I'll settle for Petros." She laughed. "No, *I* don't have a problem with him. But, well you know how he is. I don't see him meshing well with the people here, but I'll trust your judgement. All right. Love you Papa; say hi to Cordy." She waved at the screen, then put her headset down.

"We have more visitors," Jason said.

Christina stood up and walked around the desk. Despite the late hour, she was dressed elegantly in a white blouse, black trousers, and stiletto-heeled shoes. "Violet! How nice to see you again."

"Same here," she said.

"So is this a social visit? I'm afraid we have a meeting but—"

"Christina, we need your help," Nathan interrupted. He hated to be rude, but he didn't want to waste her time either. "Rather, The Agency's help."

"Nathan," Christina hissed. "You know you can't say anything about that to just anyone!" She rubbed her forehead with her fingers. "No offense, Violet. But tell me, how am I supposed to run a secret shifter protection agency when no one can keep it a secret?"

"She's my mate," Nathan blurted out. "So she's not just *anyone*." Well, that was it. The cat was out of the bag.

"Your mate?" Jason looked back and forth between Nathan and Violet. "Congrats, man!" He grabbed Nathan's hand and slapped him on the shoulder. Luke said nothing as usual and stood there, arms crossed at his chest, his tawny gold eyes observing what was happening.

"Er ..." He waited for Violet to deny it, but to his surprise she didn't say anything.

"Oh my Lord!" Christina hopped over to Violet and drew her into a hug. "That's wonderful! Tell me, have you experienced the bond yet?"

Violet stood stiffly in Christina's hug. "Well, actually—"

"Never mind. That's a personal question! But—"

"Please, Christina," Nathan said. "We really do need The Agency's help. There's a missing shifter, and she might be in danger. We have to help her."

"Oh, of course," Christina said. "That's what we do, after all. Or what we're trying to do. Let's go out into the living room. As you can see, I'm trying to set up my office here until we move into the new HQ. That should be soon as things are moving along."

Christina seemed excited talking about how they were setting up a branch of The Shifter Protection Agency in Blackstone. The Agency was the brainchild of Ari Stavros, her step-father and Alpha of the Lykos clan. He started it to help shifters in trouble all over the world.

They settled in the living room with Jason and Christina in the love seat, Nathan and Violet on the couch across from them, and Luke in the arm chair in the corner.

Christina turned to Violet. "So, tell me what's wrong. Who's missing?"

"It's Nathan's date's sister," she began.

"Excuse me?" Christina shot daggers at the wolf shifter.

Nathan put his hands up. "I swear, she wasn't my date! She was a chick I met at The Den—"

"Even worse," Christina said.

Nathan groaned. "Nothing happened. I swear. Melanie told you, I told you—"

"Can we just get on with it?" Jason asked, putting an arm around his wife.

"Right," Violet said, and she relayed the story of Melanie and Joanne to the rest of them.

"Holy shit," Jason exclaimed. "You walked into a biker bar by yourself and grabbed that man by the throat? You're one ballsy lady." He frowned and wrinkled his nose at her. "What are you anyway? A jaguar? Leopard?"

Violet seemed to ignore him. "There might be others kidnapped along with her."

"Could they be working with some kind of trafficking ring?" Nathan said. "They probably saw Joanne as a vulner-able college student, away from home where no one would check on her. Maybe they didn't even know she was a shifter, hence the struggle in her apartment."

"Will you help us?" Violet asked.

Christina's face grew serious. "Of course I want to help. And we will." She stood up. "I don't have The Agency's full resources with me right now, but I'll see what I can do. We'll think of something and by morning—"

"Morning?" Violet shot to her feet. "What do you mean morning?"

"Baby," Nathan stood up. "Christina is an expert on these things. She'll have a plan tomorrow, and we can get some rest for now."

"Rest?" Violet stood back. "Rest? How can I rest when Joanne and probably those other girls are out there in the hands of those men! God knows what's happening to them—"

"I'm sorry Violet," Christina began. "I know how you feel. But even when I was just a field agent, I was taught we had to plan these things. Do some recon and then figure out what to do so as few people as possible get hurt. I have analysts and computer experts all over the world I can deploy, but I have to be smart about how I use our resources."

Violet turned to Jason. "You're a dragon. Please, can't you help them? Just ... fly over there and scare those bikers into telling us where the girls are."

Jason shook his head. "It doesn't work that way. And I'm already in enough trouble for my last public outing."

Violet cried in frustration. "Why won't any of you do something about this?"

"Baby—"

She swiped Nathan's hand away. "No! You said we would find her and make sure she's safe."

"Be reasonable, Violet. We can't do everything tonight." Nathan sighed. "What's the matter with you?"

"Nothing," she growled.

Her face was twisted in anguish, and Nathan could see how pain much she was in. He could practically feel the animal inside of her, confused and suffering. Gone was the cold and calculated Dr. Robichaux. He didn't know how, but he knew there was something else going on here.

"Violet!" he called as she turned around and ran toward the door. "Sorry," he said to Christina and Jason. "And thanks for helping out."

He didn't wait for them to say anything. He wanted to make sure Violet didn't get too far. Sure, he drove them there in his car, but she was a shifter; she could turn into her animal and run away and he'd never catch up with her.

The elevator doors closed as he reached the hallway. "Fuck!" He took the stairs, praying to God he would make it down before she did.

As he got to the ground floor, he heard the ding of the elevator signaling its arrival. "Violet!" he called as she ran out of the lobby door.

He chased after her, catching her in the middle of the parking lot. "Violet, stop. Please. Tell me what's the matter."

She whirled around. "What's the matter?" Her eyes blazed like blue fire. "Your friends are sitting there doing *nothing* when they could help find Joanne!"

"Baby, calm down! They're not doing *nothing;* they're trying to help!" He gripped her shoulders to keep her steady. "Please. Tell me what's really wrong."

The expression on Violet's beautiful face turned from angry to agony. Her eyes filled with tears threatening to spill over. "I'm not doing this again. I'm not going to sit back and wait and let another innocent girl die. Not again!"

"Again?" Nathan could feel the pain radiating off her. "Oh God. Violet." He pulled her to him, crushing her in his arms in a fierce hug. He buried his nose in her hair. "Tell me, Violet. Tell me why you're hurting. I need to know." Because he couldn't stand seeing her like this and being unable to do anything about it.

"I ..." She took deep, calming breaths. "It was back in Eritana, when I was doing my research. We were based in this remote village, and I was staying at the girl's orphanage. They had nothing, you know? And yet they gave me a place to stay. I'm not good around kids, and they were wary of me. But, later on ... they made me ... not so lonely." She rubbed her face against his shirt, the moisture of her tears soaking the fabric. "Then, I got this job with Blackstone and it was the chance of a lifetime. I took it and resigned from the research team. The girls threw me a party the night before I was going to leave." Violet looked up at him, her cheeks streaked with dried tears. "Then the men came in the middle of the night."

Nathan's jaw set into a hard line. "Men?"

"Insurgents. Rebels. Or possibly the military themselves. I don't recall. They wanted the girls. All twenty-three of them. The oldest one was barely thirteen years old."

He wanted to ask what for, but at the same time he didn't want to know. The news was filled with stories about what happened to unprotected girls in war-torn countries. "And then what?"

"I woke up and got out of my tent. There were a dozen of them. All armed. They were pointing their guns at the girls and lining them up to place them in their truck."

"Did they ...?"

"I don't remember much, but I do remember how angry I was. How angry my tiger was. You see to us, the girls were our cubs. Ours to protect. I shifted, and then there was so much blood ... I killed most of them."

He breathed a sigh of relief. "You saved them."

"I saved twenty-two of them." She swallowed. "The truck drove away with one girl. Nadia."

"Did the authorities go after her?"

She gave a bitter laugh. "No, of course not. The village elders didn't have time to look for a girl, much less an orphaned one. And they ... they said I was a monster, and they locked me up in a cage."

"No!" Those bastards.

"Few people had heard of shifters there, so they didn't know what I was. My team had been driven away too. I didn't want to agitate the villagers, so I waited. My university has protocols in place, and I trusted the system would work."

"They got you out?"

She nodded. "Yes. But three days had passed. As soon as I was out, I hunted those men down. It only took me twenty-four hours."

He dreaded her next words, but he knew she had to say them. And he had to hear them. "Nadia?"

"G-g-gone. By the time I tracked them down to their camp ... oh God!" She sobbed. "They didn't ... touch her, but I think they didn't know what to do with her. Nadia cried a lot and maybe they got pissed off and—"

"Sshhh ... Baby, it's okay. You don't have to say any more."

"I killed as many of them as I could. I left one so they would know who I was and made sure no one messed with the girls again. They called me the Golden Demon. They said I was a monster. And I am."

"You're not," Nathan said. "You saved those girls. They're alive because of you."

She hiccuped but remained silent.

"Violet, baby ... I'm sorry. So sorry for what happened to

you and for Nadia. You got your revenge. And I know you want to find Joanne too, but lashing out like this won't help. Tiring yourself out won't help, either. We need to get some rest and start fresh in the morning."

"But—"

He planted a quick kiss on her lips. "I promise you, we will find her."

"I want to believe that," she said, laying her head on his chest. "But I want to do something now."

"We are doing—"

Someone clearing their throat interrupted him. When Nathan looked up, he saw Luke standing a few feet away from them.

"For what it's worth," he began, "I completely disagree with Jason and Christina's plan."

"You do?"

He nodded. "And I told them that. That's why I'm here."

Violet pulled away from Nathan. "I don't understand."

"Christina wants to recruit me to be part of The Agency," Luke explained. "I thought, why the hell not? Especially if it means we get to catch the bastards who tried to do us in during the wedding. I already do my patrols every night. She only asked that I do a more organized approach, move in grids, and report back any unusual activity."

"Wow." Nathan had to admit that was a genius plan.

"Anyway, like I said, if someone's got your friend, then we shouldn't be sitting on our hands doing nothing."

"Wait. Are you saying you want to help?"

He nodded. "Yeah. Sounds like you two have been running around the whole day. Get some rest, and I'll take over from here." He rubbed his jaw with his fingers. "So, that bar. The Bitter End?"

Violet nodded. "Off Highway 54, north of Verona Mills. What are you going to do?"

"I'll head there and keep watch. Follow them and tell you what I find."

Violet seemed satisfied with his answer. "Thank you, Luke. That would help me sleep better."

He shrugged. "I'll call you if I find anything." Without another word, he walked away.

"Your friend is ... different," Violet said.

Nathan chuckled. "Yeah, that describes Luke all right. But, like he said, let's get some rest." He took her elbow and walked her back toward Jason and Christina's apartment building.

"Your car is over there." Violet pointed to the Mustang as they walked past it.

"I know," he said as he led her to the building next to Jason's. "We're not going to my car." He fished for his keys and opened the door to the lobby. "We're going to my loft."

"Your loft? You live here too?" she asked. "But—"

"Violet, it's late. And we're both tired. I don't want to drive you all the way back to the hotel." He gently guided her into the elevator.

"I can get a cab—"

"And Luke doesn't have your number, he has mine. He's going to call me when he finds something. Do you want to waste precious time driving back and forth from here to your hotel when he does?"

"I suppose you're right."

They were already in front of his apartment door. "Don't worry; I've got three bedrooms. I'll lend you some clothes, you can have a hot bath, and then sleep."

She sighed in defeat. "That sounds good, actually."

He kissed the top of her head. For a second he thought

she'd recoil, but she leaned into him. "Okay, bedroom's on the right, same place as Christina's office. You'll find everything you need in the closet."

"Thank you," she said, pulling away from him.

Nathan watched her disappear down the hallway. When he heard the door close, he walked back to the living room, sank down on the couch, and placed his face in his hands.

"Christ." This morning seemed like a million years ago. He'd been hurt by her words in the trailer, but now ... he couldn't even recall the feeling.

Violet. She was so strong. Not just physically, but mentally and emotionally. After what happened to her, a lesser man would have crumbled. But she didn't. She picked up the pieces and went on with her life. It must be hard to compartmentalize like that.

It all clicked into place. Why Violet was the way she was. She had to keep her emotions packed away, or, he guessed, the survivor's guilt would consume her. He saw her crack today. Before this whole mess, he wanted to see her show some emotion but not like this. He was glad she had the cold and calculated Dr. Robichaux persona to protect her.

"Nathan?"

"Huh?" How long had he been sitting there? A while probably. Violet was standing in the doorway. Her hair was wet, and she was wearing one of his spare shirts which came down to her knees. "Everything okay? Do you need some water or anything?"

She shook her head. "It's too quiet in the room."

"Oh."

"Can I stay out here? With you? Maybe we can watch TV or something?"

"Of course." He gestured to the spot beside him on the

sofa, then reached for the TV remote. "Anything in particular you want to watch?"

She sat down, bringing her knees up to her chest. "It doesn't matter."

He scrolled through the channels, then settled on an old movie musical starring the actress from *The Wizard of Oz* singing a song about a trolley.

Violet watched the movie quietly, not saying a thing. He tried to glance at her once in a while, unable to concentrate. How could he when she was so close to him that her scent was driving him wild? Or rather, it was her scent mixed in with his body wash. It made him think of getting her into his bathroom and using the detachable shower head in creative ways.

Get a grip. She'd already been through so much today. They both had. She didn't need him getting all horny around her. It had riled him up, knowing what happened to her. Sure, that was before they knew each other, but he had the instinct to protect her from everything. She was far away from those people who caged her. That was the past, and she'd never have to see them again.

As the credits started to roll, Nathan felt something brush up against him. It was Violet. She had fallen asleep and slumped over on him, her thick damp hair tickling his skin. With a resigned sigh, he put an arm around her, pulled her close, and switched the TV to the sports channel, turning the volume low so as not to disturb Violet. She snuggled against him, burying her face into his side. His wolf sighed in contentment, happy that Violet was comfortable enough to let her guard down around them.

Yeah buddy, he thought. *Me too.*

CHAPTER TEN

As LIGHT FILTERED through her closed eyelids, Violet's first thought was that the firm mattress she was sleeping on was moving.

No, not moving. *Breathing.*

Her eyes opened, slowly at first. She had to blink a few times, but she didn't need to see to know where she was. Nathan's masculine scent was all over her, and she wasn't on a firm mattress but rather, his rock hard body.

Oh my.

Violet wanted to move away. She really did, except she didn't want to disturb him. She was comfortable right where she was. Pressing her nose against his shirt, she took in another whiff.

"That's adorable."

"Huh?" She looked up at him.

One green eye was open, peering down at her. "The purring."

"What?" A hand went up to her chest, feeling the vibrations. She *was* purring. "Oh!"

Her cheeks went hot, but when she tried to move away, strong arms wrapped around her. Nathan rolled her over, so her back was on the couch and he was on top.

She stared up at him, watching as his gaze roved and lazily appraised her face. Reaching up, she touched the stubble that had grown on his otherwise clean-shaven jaw. He turned and pressed his lips to her fingers, the touch sending a mild shock through her.

When he lowered his head to hers, she didn't protest. In fact, the only thing she could think of was how nice it felt. His delicious kisses sent thrills through her, and when his tongue traced her lips, she opened herself to him eagerly.

Nathan settled between her legs, pressing his hardness against her mound. Her pussy grew wet, and he let out a groan. The only thing between them was her damp panties and his boxer briefs. Adjusting the angle of his hips, he positioned the ridge of his cock just right so it hit her clit.

She moaned his name against his mouth and dug her fingers into his scalp. He responded by pulling up the shirt she was wearing and cupping a breast. She didn't think this could feel any better, until his thumb brushed her nipple sending her spiraling into an orgasm.

She threw her head back as her body convulsed. His lips clamped onto her neck, his teeth grazing at the skin there, sucking and biting just enough to feel good without breaking the skin.

"Nathan," she whispered as she relaxed. There it was again. The purring. Her tiger was calm and peaceful and happy. And so was she. It all felt normal, and though the events of yesterday was still on her mind, she wasn't as angry or hurt.

She opened her eyes, and he was staring down at her

"You have beautiful eyes, you know," he said, stroking her cheek. "Light blue with a ring of dark navy."

"It's a form of heterochromia. A mutation."

He chuckled softly. "My beautiful little mutant."

She gave him a tight smile. *Ironic.*

"So, tiger, huh?" he said with a grin.

"Kind of," she said.

"Hmmm?"

"Nathan …" Hoping to distract him, she reached her hand down between them, slipping over his rock hard abs to the growing bulge between his legs.

"Baby," he groaned as her fingers stroked him over his underwear. "I swear when I smelled you getting wet, I nearly came."

"Oh?" She pressed the heel of her palm against him.

"Fffuuck." He moved his hips, thrusting his cock against her. "That feels so good. Which is why I have to do this." He stopped and wrapped a hand around her wrist. He pulled them up, so they were sitting on the couch. "Violet, we can't do this. Not—"

Her chest stopped vibrating, and she recoiled. "It's fine," she said, her voice going flat.

Before she could stand up, he grabbed her hands. "Violet, listen to me."

"I said it's fine. You already told me you don't want me."

"Goddamnit!" He let out a frustrated groan. "This is why we can't have sex. There's so much we need to talk about."

She looked at him, stunned by his words. Her usual cool mask slipped on. "What is there to talk about? Unless you don't really want—"

"Stop throwing my words in my face, dammit." He ran a

hand through his hair. "Can't you see how muddy things are between us? I was about to explain everything to you last night when Melanie showed up. We need to sort things out before we jump into bed."

She crossed her arms over her chest. "That's rich coming from someone who's 'drowning in so much pussy'," she sneered. When Nathan's face faltered, she instantly regretted her words. "Nathan—"

A soft *brrrrr* sound made them both stop and turn their heads. Nathan's phone was dancing on the coffee table. With a frustrated grunt, he grabbed it.

"Hello ... yeah ... okay. Text me the location. We'll be there." He tossed the phone on the couch. "Get dressed," he said, his tone clipped.

"Nathan? I'm so—"

"I'll meet you out here in five," he said, then turned his back to her.

She watched him walk up the stairs and disappear into the door of what she assumed was his bedroom. Her heart grew heavy, and she felt her stomach drop all the way to her knees.

Damn her stupid emotions! Why was she acting like this? His actions and words confused the hell out of her, that's why. Combined with the emotional rollercoaster that was yesterday ...

She refused to give into her feelings. Even though her tiger was whimpering with hurt, she took it and locked it away. She was in charge here. And she refused to let Nathan Caldwell control what she was feeling. Not when there was work to be done.

We have to save her, she told her tiger. *Save Joanne. Because we couldn't save Nadia.*

Her tiger roared in fury and its claws came out, like it

always did when it remembered what happened to the little girl. Their adopted little cub.

Don't worry, she told it as she made her way back to the guest room. *You'll have your chance to use those claws.*

————————

The car ride was silent and tense. Not that Violet expected anything different. Nathan had been waiting for her when she came out to the living room. He didn't even say anything, just walked out the door. Didn't look at her, didn't acknowledge her presence. Instead, his steely gaze stared straight ahead. He didn't even protest when she got into the car.

Violet wasn't expecting riveting conversation but to pretend she didn't exist was going too far. For God's sake, he was the one who turned her down for sex again and *he* was mad? He kissed her first. She didn't proposition him this time, so he didn't have any excuse.

I'm not making that mistake again. Sure, he was hot. Those eyes could melt her panties away, and that body ... and his cock, so thick and hard under her palms. *Stop!*

She was just frustrated. Maybe after all this was done, she'd have a session or five with her Battery Operated Boyfriend. At least BOB never let her down.

The Mustang screeched to a halt, and Violet jolted forward, the seatbelt digging across her chest. She looked outside. "Where are we?"

The sound of the slamming door was her answer. "Real mature, Nathan," she mumbled under her breath as she nearly tore the buckle off.

As she stepped out of the car, she looked around them. They had stopped on the side of the highway in a small lay-by.

Luke was standing off to the side, his feet planted apart and his tattooed arms crossed over his wide chest. Violet shivered when their gazes clashed, and her tiger shrank back. His lion – what else could he be with those long blond locks? – was so dominant, she wondered how any other shifter could even stand to be in his presence for long periods of time. It made her uncomfortable just being next to him, let alone when he turned those tawny golden eyes on her.

"Well, we're here," Nathan said as he kicked a pebble out of his way. "What do you have?"

"I staked out the bar 'till closing time. Then I followed the bikers to their compound." Luke nodded behind him. "It's about half a mile that way. They were up all night, so I don't think they're awake or sober yet."

"We should go check it out," Nathan said. He brushed past Violet and disappeared into the trees.

Luke gestured for her to go ahead. "I'll take up the rear."

"Thanks."

She followed behind Nathan, keeping her distance, but not too much that Luke had to slow down. At least neither Luke nor Nathan made her stay behind in the car. She was ready to fight them tooth and claw for her right to be here.

Nathan stopped and put his hand up, and Violet nearly collided into him because she wasn't paying attention. He shot her a dirty look.

"That it?" Nathan asked and Luke nodded.

The compound was surrounded by a barbed-wire fence that was twelve feet high. From this angle, she could only see one large structure that looked like it had several rooms continuously added to it like some type of Frankenbuilding.

"Not quite up to building code," Nathan said in a low voice. "So, what did you learn, Luke?"

"After The Bitter End closed, I saw the Kings bring out two guys, both tied up. Probably your kidnappers. Tossed 'em into a van and they all drove out here."

"Then?"

"There was lots of partying. More alcohol, drinking, girls. Then, lots of screaming."

"Screaming?" Violet asked.

"They took the two men into the back room," he nodded to the structure closest to them, "and worked them over. They got a good beating. Probably passed out a couple of times, then got woken up so they could start all over again."

Violet gasped. "Are they dead?"

"No. Still alive. Before I came to get you guys, I could still hear 'em breathing and moaning."

"Is that fence electrified?" Nathan asked.

"Yep. I could jump over it and turn off the alarm."

"Sounds like a plan," Nathan said.

"I should do it," Violet interjected.

"You?" Luke asked.

"Yes," she said, reaching for the top button of her shirt.

Nathan's face turned red. "Luke will do it," he said in a tight voice.

"Why? Tigers have a higher vertical leap than lions."

"If we were equally matched," Luke countered. "You could jump twelve feet, max. That's still not enough to get over that fence without getting barbecued."

She gritted her teeth. "I once got over a brick wall that was fifteen feet high. When was the last time you had to do that?" When neither men said anything, she let out a frustrated groan. "What's the plan anyway, gentlemen? Once I turn off the fence, then what? Are you going to storm in? Or quietly take their prisoners and interrogate them?"

When they didn't answer, she puffed out an angry breath. This was just like last night when she and Melanie were waiting in the car. Nathan said he'd get the information they needed, but they'd been sitting out there for twenty minutes and she had grown frustrated. "Men," she groaned, then turned around.

"Violet!" Nathan hissed, but she ignored him as she sprinted away.

The barbed wire fence went all the way to the front gate. It was closed and one guy sat in a chair, playing with his phone, seemingly guarding the compound. She walked closer to him and called his attention. "Excuse me."

The guard—a young man who didn't look older than twenty—looked up from his phone. His eyes widened when he saw her and he quickly got to his feet. "Whaddaya want, lady?" he asked, his voice sounding like he was barely past puberty.

She raised a brow at him. "I need to see Prez, young man."

He let out a chuckle. "No one can just walk up here and asks for Prez. Whaddaya think this is? A fucking information desk at the mall?"

Unperturbed, she walked closer, her nose almost touching the gate. "Tell him the shifter from last night is here." She brought her tiger to the surface, flashing its glowing cat eyes at him.

The man gulped audibly. "Jesus, you for real, lady? I thought they were all joshin' me when they told me about the crazy shifter lady who beat up Ruiz!"

"I assure you I'm very real." She opened her mouth and bared her fangs at him.

He jumped back. "F-fine! I'll tell Prez, but I can't guarantee he'll want to see you." He turned tail and disappeared into the building behind him.

"Violet, Goddamnit!"

Nathan ran up to her, then stopped a few inches from where she was standing. Luke was behind him, casually strolling toward them, the expression on his face unreadable. "What the fuck are you up to? Don't you know these men are dangerous? What do you think you're going to do? Just walk up here and then they'll open the gate and welcome you?"

As if on cue, there was a loud click followed by a motorized whirring as the gates swung open.

Violet gave him a smug look. "I guess so." As she turned to walk into the compound, a hand on her elbow stopped her.

"Violet, wait."

"I'm done waiting," she said without looking back. "You can wait. Or you can follow me. Your choice." She continued walking inside, ignoring Nathan's curses as he caught up to her.

"In there," the young guard said, pointing to the door that led into the main building.

"Thank you." Her parents had raised her to be polite after all.

The first thing Violet noticed about the inside of the Kings of Death compound was the smell. Unwashed bodies, alcohol, smoke, weed, and God-knows-what else. It took every ounce of her strength not to gag.

The bikers definitely had a wild party last night based on the empty bottles of liquor, broken furniture, and passed out people in various states of undress all over the floor. She stepped over a snoring man who was only wearing boxer shorts on her way to the pool table where Prez and a few of his men were gathering.

"Look who's here," Prez said. He was shirtless, his hair sticking up and his eyes bloodshot. "Remember when I told you this chick had the balls the size of melons? Forget what I said; they're the size of fucking Kansas." The men behind him laughed. "So, lady, what brings you here? I'm sure it's not the company."

"I need to talk to your men. The ones who kidnapped those girls."

He took a pull from his beer bottle. "You don't give up, do you? How do you know they're still alive? We could have buried them somewhere and you'll never find 'em."

"I can hear them breathing," she lied. Technically Luke did, but he didn't have to know that.

"Shit." Prez put the bottle down. "I don't know why, but I like ya, lady. Maybe it's cuz you could probably shred me to pieces with your pretty little claws."

"I *could*," she said.

"Good thing you got me while I'm in a good mood. I've had my morning beer, smoked some dope, had some pussy."

"Sounds like a busy morning."

He laughed. "All right. If it'll get you and your girlfriends," he motioned to Nathan and Luke, "off my back, you can have a couple minutes with them." He nodded to his men. "Go get those bastards outta the tank and bring 'em here."

Violet didn't let her guard down. Beside her, neither did Luke and Nathan. She was glad they were keeping their mouths shut even though she could feel the tension from both men. Prez was allowing her to stay in control, at least for now.

"Here they are," Prez said as four of his bikers dragged the men in. They dumped their bloody, limp bodies on the floor. One guy walked to the fridge, got a bottle of water, and dumped it on their faces.

"Prez! I'm sorry!" Ellis, the younger one shouted as he came to consciousness. His face was bloody, his upper lip split, and one eye closed shut. "I swear, it was all Ruiz's idea!"

"Fucking rat!" Ruiz roared, wiping water from his face which was in an even worse state than Ellis's. He looked up at Violet. "I ain't talking."

"Who paid you to kidnap them?" Nathan asked.

"I-I-I don't know who," Ellis said. "It was Ruiz's contact. He said it was ten grand per girl, and we could split it if I helped."

"Where'd you stash them?" Nathan asked.

Ellis looked at Ruiz, who gave him a death glare. When he shut his mouth, Nathan reached down and grabbed him by the neck. "You know I can snap your spine in half and eat you whole, right?" He bared his canines at Ellis and let out a growl that was pure wolf.

"P-p-please no!"

The acidic smell of urine assaulted Violet's nose. "Are they still alive?" she asked.

"They were when we delivered them. The guy gave us this medicine, right? And told us to inject them to make sure they didn't shift into their animals. But they weren't dangerous or anything; no bears or wolves or anythin' with teeth. That last girl, I saw her grow wings. Ruiz struggled with her because she was tryin' to fight back, and I didn't have the stuff ready. Anyway, after we grab 'em, we bring them to this warehouse."

"Where?" Luke asked.

"I-i-t's the old canning factory at the edge of town. Right by the old 79."

Luke and Nathan looked at each other. Violet knew something was up. She turned to Prez. "Thank you for all your help. We'll be headed out now."

Prez laughed, then his face turned serious. "I'd invite you to come back, but I don't want any more trouble."

"I promise I shall never darken your door again," Violet said as she pivoted on her heel and walked out. By the time she, Nathan, and Luke were out of the compound and the gate shut behind them, her heart rate had mostly returned to normal.

"That was stupid and reckless!" Nathan roared. "What the fuck were you thinking?"

"Don't cuss at me," she bit back. "And I got things done, right? Besides, I knew they weren't going to hurt me. They said they don't hurt women and children."

"That's not the point!" Nathan gripped her arms. "Walking into dangerous situations can get you killed!"

Violet shrugged his hands off. "I'm still alive and I've survived far worse! Stop acting like you care about what happens to me, especially after the way you've treated me this entire morning."

"For God's sake—"

"Can we can the personal shit for a second?" Luke asked with a snort of annoyance.

A sobering wave washed over her. "Right. We should go check out that old factory then." A look passed between Luke and Nathan again. "There's something else, isn't there? What aren't you telling me?"

Nathan nodded at Luke. "You heard what he said, right?"

"Oh yeah."

"What?" Violet asked.

"He said they had to inject those girls with something. To stop them from shifting."

She shrugged. "Seems logical to me." There were a few substances that could incapacitate a shifter or even suppress their animals for a short time. They were all expensive and difficult to obtain, but she doubted that was a problem for anyone who could afford to pay ten thousand dollars per kidnapping.

"Initially, I thought these guys were after girls in general," Nathan said.

What he was saying struck her. "You mean ... someone paid those men to kidnap shifters?"

Luke's face went grim. "Sounds like it."

"Whatever for?"

"Who the fuck knows?" Nathan's fingers tightened into fists. "These bastards ... they could be connected to whoever's been causing trouble for us. Someone already tried to blow up Matthew and Catherine's wedding."

"And that's why Ari Stavros and Hank are putting up a branch of The Agency in Blackstone," Luke added. "There's a group of people out there who wants all shifters gone."

Violet's mind went through the list of known anti-shifter groups. "Who could it be? SPHK? Humans First?"

"None of the usual suspects," Nathan said with a shake of his head. "Bigger. And they're not lobbying to take away our rights or holding up hate signs at rallies."

"They're out to eliminate us," Luke finished.

Violet felt the blood drain from her face. "How ..."

"Christina's been sharing her intelligence with us," Nathan said. "She wants to make sure we're informed, especially with her still getting things settled. When Hank gathered us and told his plan, we said we'd all pitch in. Me, Matthew, Jason of course, Ben, Luke, as well as Sybil and Kate."

"But how can you be sure it's them?"

Nathan's face grew dark. "That canning factory Ellis was talking about? That used to be owned by Hank Lennox's father. One day, the county just decided to move the town line, so it was right in the middle of the factory. The people of Verona Mills got all up in arms about having a dragon shifter owning something in their town, so he had to shut it down."

Luke's mouth tightened into a straight line. "If these guys put one of their headquarters at the town line, and in one of the old Lennox factories, you know they're planning something big with Blackstone."

"Not to mention the biggest 'fuck you' to the Lennoxes," Nathan added.

"These guys don't mess around," Luke said. "Which is why we need to call Christina and Jason now and see what they say."

"We can't just stand around waiting for them," Violet said, the urgency in her voice evident.

"We can't expose ourselves and what we know. We'd blow Christina's operation and alert this group to our plans."

"I don't care," Violet said. "I'm going to that warehouse, and you two can sit here and twiddle your thumbs."

"And we need to go higher up the food chain," Luke said, "so we can put these bastards away." He put his hands on his hips and loomed over Violet.

Her tiger hissed but shrank back when it felt Luke's lion roar at her.

"Stop," Nathan said, his eyes glowing. "Luke, I swear to God, if you keep doing that to her I'm going to tear you a new asshole."

"I can do that by myself, thank you," Violet said, scrunching up every piece of courage she had.

"For fuck's sake!" Nathan let out a frustrated growl. "Look, why don't we drive over there, gather intel, and call Christina and Jason on the way?"

It's a good compromise, Violet thought begrudgingly. "Fine. Let's go." But she wasn't going to make any promises about staying put until they got back up. If she found out Joanne or any other innocent shifter was in there being held against their will, she was going to save them—with or without Nathan and Luke's help.

CHAPTER ELEVEN

Nᴀᴛʜᴀɴ ᴡᴀs sᴛɪʟʟ ꜰᴜᴍɪɴɢ as they neared the old canning factory. *Goddamn stubborn woman.* He couldn't believe she would pull that stunt. When she walked away from him and headed to the entrance of the biker compound, his heart stopped. He nearly tore Luke to pieces for trying to prevent him from going after her. Relief had swept over him when they came out of the compound, knowing she was safe. If anything had happened to her, he would never forgive himself.

And so he was now back to being mad at her for this morning. After all they'd been through, she was still throwing his words right back in his face, rubbing it in about what he said about having other women. Didn't she realize she wasn't one of them? That the reason he didn't want to just have sex with her was because it wasn't going to be a one night thing? He wanted to clear the air so they could start fresh.

How could she even think he didn't want her? He made her come twice now, and she only had to look at him and he was as hard as a hammer. Is this what being mates was about? He felt sorry for his friends. Maybe he should just be happy being single the rest of his life. Glancing over at Luke, he thought it wouldn't be so bad. He and Luke could be the confirmed bachelors of the group. The fun uncles. Well, he could be the fun uncle and Luke can be grumpy uncle. Of course, if Luke found his own mate first and left him alone, Nathan would probably hang himself at the injustice of it all.

"We should stop here," Luke said. They were still about a mile away. "We can hide the car and go the long way 'round."

"Do you know the exact location of the factory?" Nathan asked.

"I think I remember. Hank took me, Jason, and Matthew hiking in this area when we were kids. He stopped to show us the old factory. It was definitely abandoned then."

Highway 79 was the old country highway that ran between Verona Mills and Blackstone. It was one of those single-lane highways that had become abandoned over the years as the wider and newer roadways were built. They didn't see any cars as they drove up the old road. Few people took it, and many of the businesses that catered to drivers on the old highway simply shut down or moved away.

They found a small clearing off the main road and parked the car there. Because of the Mustang's bright color, they had to gather some discarded branches to cover it. Nathan winced thinking about the scratches on the paint job, but he knew in the grand scheme of things it would be a minor inconvenience.

Luke led them up the highway, then turned off onto a side road. He veered off on another path, and a few minutes later he raised his hand to signal them to stop. "It's right up ahead. Get down."

The ground was a gentle upward slope, so it was easy to get on their bellies and see the old factory standing about twenty feet away from them. The structure was old and made of wood but still standing, if a little run down. From the outside, it looked just like any abandoned building. However, someone had built a barbed wire fence around it.

"Good news is the fence isn't as high as the one in the compound," Luke said.

"The bad news?"

"It's got about a thousand times more power," Violet said as she cringed and put her hands over her ears. "It could probably burn anyone who touched it into a crisp."

"What's wrong?" Nathan frowned.

"The frequency of the electric fence is really annoying," Luke said.

Ah, right. Felines could hear higher frequencies than other shifters. "What do we do?"

Luke slowly got up and began to unbutton his shirt. "I'll jump over and turn it off. She'll know when I've done it, and you two cut your way in." He pointed to the rear of the building. "If I remember correctly, there's a service door in the back. Let's meet there."

"Good idea," Nathan thought, glad Luke volunteered first. As much as he was curious about Violet's animal, he wasn't too crazy about anyone else seeing her naked. And of course, it would be better if Luke got caught than her. Who knew what he'd do if he saw anyone touching Violet.

Luke walked into the group of trees behind them. The sound of paws thumping on the ground told him he had already shifted. All they had to do now was wait.

He glanced over at Violet. She still had a pained expression on her face. "Baby, you okay?" he whispered. "Why don't you think of something else to distract you?"

"Can't. Have to listen."

Seeing her uncomfortable like this made his insides turn, but he knew she was right. Not sure what else to do, he placed a hand on her back and gently stroked it. She relaxed a little bit, her mouth parting in a sigh.

A few minutes later, Violet let out the breath she'd been holding. "It's done," she said.

They moved quickly, crossing the distance to the fence within seconds. Nathan already had this claws out, and he slashed a hole, one large enough for them to get through. He helped Violet inside first, then followed her as they ran to the factory. They pressed themselves against the wall, waiting for Luke.

"You made it." Luke appeared next to them, wearing only his jeans, his hair in disarray around his shoulders. "I did a quick look around, no guards or anything outside. Not visible anyway."

"Their best security is keeping a low profile and not attracting any attention," Nathan guessed. "What do we do now?" Maybe they should have thought this through a little more.

Luke closed his eyes. "I can hear … people in there. Walking around. And sound bouncing off the walls. This place was basically a shell when I saw it. They've been busy doing construction inside."

"And lab equipment?" Violet's delicate brows wrinkled. "Reminds me of when I walked past the biology lab at my university. Cages opening and closing. Glass tubes and beakers moving around. A centrifuge running." She shivered visibly.

"No guards outside, probably not a lot inside, either," Nathan said. The place was well-hidden, so the fence should have been enough to keep anyone out.

"I'll go in and look around," Luke said. "Nathan can be my backup. Violet, you should head back out and wait for Jason and Christina. They're on their way."

"No," Violet said. "I'm staying here."

Nathan was losing his patience. "For fuck—crying out loud, Violet, just listen to us this once!" He was going to tie her up and carry her out himself if he had to.

"I'm not leaving," she said. "And that's—"

A piercing scream in the air interrupted them. "*He's just a child!*" The woman's voice was loud and clear.

Nathan felt his blood run cold. "You said there was lab equipment in there?"

Violet nodded slowly, her nostrils flaring and her eyes glowing in anger.

"Fuck." It clicked into place. What this was. They were experimenting on shifters. And right under their very noses. The look on Luke's and Violet's faces told him they came to the same conclusion.

"We need to get those people out," Violet said. "It's not just about Joanne anymore."

"And the bastards in charge will go down," Luke said.

"What's the ETA on Christina and Jason?" Nathan asked. "We need to come up with a plan."

Another scream—this time a child's—rang through the air. It sent chills down Nathan's spine.

Violet's face turned into a mask of pure rage.

"Violet." He was about to place a hand on her, but she was too fast. The back door blew open and she was gone.

"Fuck," Luke cursed. "Let's go before she gets herself killed."

He didn't even wait for Luke. His wolf was screaming at him to protect Violet at all costs.

The inside of the building was nothing like the outside. White walls and white fluorescent lamps covered the interior. The antiseptic smell reminded him of a hospital. He sniffed the air, searching for her scent, following it until he came to an open door. Violet was in the middle of the laboratory standing over a figure lying on a table.

"Don't you ever do that again," he said, keeping his hands at his side to stop himself from pulling her into his arms.

She looked up at him, eyes still blazing. "It's her. Joanne."

The woman on the bed looked pale and her eyes were closed, but he recognized the scent. Her body lay still, but the rise and fall of her chest told him she was alive. She was wearing a white hospital gown and various wires were stuck under the paper-thin fabric. Violet made quick work of them, pulling them off her.

A moan caught his attention. There was a second table behind Violet where another girl was lying down. He strode over to her and checked for a pulse.

"Is she okay?" Violet asked.

"Heartbeat's faint, but she seems to be hanging in there." He brushed aside a lock of hair and let out a curse under his breath. She smelled like fur, probably a deer, and she didn't look older than sixteen. Luke was already carrying Joanne in his arms, so he gently lifted the young girl up.

"Let's get them out of here," Luke said.

As they walked out of the lab, a loud siren began to ring out and the lights flickered and flashed red.

"Shit! They know we're here."

"Had to happen eventually," Luke said. "C'mon. We need to get out in case they have lockdown procedures."

They turned to the exit but Violet remained very still. "Someone's down there." She pointed in the opposite direction. "She needs our help!"

"We'll come back for her! Let's go now and save these two," Nathan urged.

"No! I'm not leaving anyone behind!" Violet pivoted and began to walk away.

"Goddamnit!" He handed the girl in his arms to Luke. "Get them out of here!"

The shouts and the sound of boots pounding on the floor coming toward them were unmistakable. Two men dressed in all black and combat gear were storming down the hallway and raising their guns as Violet came closer.

"No!" Nathan growled. His wolf ripped out of his body as he made a run for her.

Violet was so quick, he would have missed it if it wasn't for his shifter senses. Her body grew to twice its size and fur rippled across her skin as she leapt into the air. And her tiger —it was unlike anything he'd ever seen before. It had faint stripes over its back running down to its tail, but the rest of its fur faded from a dark strawberry blonde to white at its paws.

The tiger landed right on one of the men, and Nathan could hear Violet's growls and the sound of teeth ripping through fabric. Nathan quickly turned his wolf's body to take down the other man. His paws swiped at the gun, sending it skidding to the ground as his massive body collided with the guard, taking him down. Opening his jaws he went right for the guys' arm and shoulder, his mouth filling with blood as his teeth sank into flesh and bone. His screams joined that of the other man.

He pulled the wolf back, knowing they had hurt the guard enough to incapacitate him. Looking over his shoulder, he saw Violet was done too. The tiger brushed past him and Violet's unusual blue eyes flickered at him before it broke into a run. She was headed for the room at the end of the hall.

He followed her as she leapt at the door, knocking it down.

The sirens had quieted, but an eerie feeling settled over Nathan. It made his wolf's hackles raise. This room was larger than the previous one they had been in and circular in shape, with different types of medical equipment and operating tables. Several cages lined one side, empty from what Nathan could spy, but the mixed smells of fur, feathers, scales, and various scents told them they weren't always so.

The man in the middle was tall and pale. He was dressed in surgical attire, his mask lowered down to his chin. He also had his arm around a dark-haired woman and held a scalpel to her neck. Behind him, a man dressed in the same combat gear as the guards in the hallway stood, his gun cocked and pointing right at Violet.

"You filthy animals! Change back or else!" He pressed the scalpel to the woman's neck, breaking the skin so a drop of blood appeared on the tip of the blade. She let out a sharp breath.

Violet's tiger let out an angry roar, but her body began to shrink. Nathan did the same, tucking his wolf away for now.

"Who are you?" Nathan said as the last of his fur receded into his skin and his snout pushed back into his head.

"And what are you doing with these shifters?" Violet asked, her voice shaky with anger.

"None of this concerns you, you abominations!" he shouted. "How dare you anyway? Walking into my lab? How did you get in here?" He let out a frustrated sound. "I told The

Chief I needed more security here! It's not like we didn't have enough to spare. Damn him and his paranoia. We need to leave now."

The woman in his arms struggled, and he tightened his grip. "Don't move Georgina, my dear. Besides, when you're gone, who's going to protect little Grayson from The Chief?"

"You monster!" she hissed. "Don't you dare!"

"The only thing that's keeping The Chief from killing him is because I deem him useful in our experiments. Otherwise, you know that boy would be gone in an instant!"

Tears flowed down her cheeks. "Please, Dr. Mendle … don't."

Dr. Mendle looked at Nathan and Violet. "Now, if you don't mind, I'll be headed out." He shook his head as Violet stepped forward. "Uh-huh. Don't take another step." He tsked, and his eyes roamed over her body. "A golden tiger. One of nature's most beautiful mutations. I would have loved to study your DNA."

Nathan gritted his teeth. "You won't get away with this. Any of this!"

"Oh really?" Dr. Mendle sneered. "Who's going to stop me? The Agency? Oh, you seem surprised. Yes, we know all about Ari Stavros' little group. He's merely a thorn in our side, of course. It was such a coincidence that we had started running this lab the moment he decided to team up with Hank Lennox to expand his club here. Not that it matters. Our organization is larger and far-reaching, and we will stamp out every last one of you!"

"Why are you in Blackstone?" Nathan asked.

"Well, technically, we're not, are we?" Mendle pointed out. "This was the perfect location for our lab since it was easy enough to find lowlifes to kidnap shifters living in the area.

Plus, with Verona Mills P.D. deep in our pockets, they would easily lose a file or two or turn their heads the other way if anyone reported anything."

"You are a monster!" Violet shrieked. "I'm going to—" Her claws came out.

"Not if you want an innocent life on your hands," Dr. Mendle warned as he pushed the scalpel deeper into Georgina's neck. Rivulets of blood flowed out. "She's a human, by the way," he spat. "So no healing for her."

"Violet," Nathan said. "Don't move."

"Yes, indeed. Stay where you are." Dr. Mendle slowly moved sideways, his guard following him as they kept their backs to the wall, getting closer to the exit.

"Stay here," he said to the guard. "Keep close to the woman. Make sure they don't move while we make our escape." The guard nodded and crossed the room to where Violet was standing, the nose of his gun pointed at her chest.

"No!" Georgina screamed. "Grayson! We can't leave him." She struggled against Mendle, then stamped her heel on his foot.

"You stupid whore!" Dr. Mendle made a grab for Georgina as she broke free of his grasp, the scalpel swinging wildly in the air.

"Bastard!" Nathan leapt in between them, intending to shield the human woman. A loud crash from behind made Mendle stop short. "What the—"

Something large and hairy with big claws shot out from the doorway. *Luke.*

The lion landed on Dr. Mendle and in a split second, Nathan grasped Georgina by the arm and shoved her out of the way just before the lion and Dr. Mendle landed on the floor. The man screamed as the lion's maw came down on his head. Then silence.

"Are you—"

The sound of a gunshot made his blood run cold, and he whipped his head around.

Violet, half-shifted, was struggling with the lone guard. Fur and teeth sprouted from her face, and her clawed hands fought for control of the rifle. The guard gave a strong push and sent Violet tumbling back into a shelf of glass bottles.

"Violet!" His blood pumped into his veins as he pushed his wolf down. No, *he* would kill this bastard with his bare hands for hurting her.

The guard wasn't expecting him, and Nathan seized him from behind and swung him around as his fist connected with his jaw. The man staggered back and Nathan leapt on top of him, pummeling his face with fury.

"Nathan ... Nathan, stop!"

His hands were like raw hamburger, red and bloodied. But the man's face was worse, and blood spurted from his mouth. The rage didn't go away, especially when his eyes landed on Violet.

She was barely standing up, her face bleeding from small cuts. Bits of glass were in her hair and skin, and a large piece was sticking out of her shoulder. Placing her fingers around the piece, she pulled it out and tossed it aside.

"Fuck!" Nathan got up and walked to her, grabbing a lab coat hanging on the wall. "Violet ..." His insides twisted, seeing her bloody and hurt like this.

"I'm fine," she choked out. "Give me a few minutes. I've already stopped bleeding." She nodded behind him. "Just help her. Please."

Georgina was standing by the cages, rattling them frantically as she sobbed. Nathan didn't want to leave her side, but his mate could be stubborn. "Put this on," he said before striding over the Georgina.

"Please get him out," she pleaded as she turned her tear-stained face to him.

Nathan bent down to peer into the small cage. Two small glowing eyes stared back at him. Using his claws, he slashed at the lock on the cage and the door swung open.

"Grayson!" Georgina pushed him aside and reached into the cage, taking out the small furry bundle. "Oh, Grayson. It's okay. Mommy's here."

The bear cub rubbed its snout against her shoulder. Its dark fur began to recede, and the body grew smaller. A little boy, probably no more than four or five, clung to Georgina as if his life depended on it.

"Mommy," he rasped. "The bad man ... is he gone?"

"He won't hurt you anymore."

A soft growl from behind made Nathan turn his head. "Luke, you okay, man?"

Luke's gaze was fixed on Georgina and her son, and the gold of his eyes was barely visible as his pupils blew up. His body tensed for a moment, and he turned away.

"Luke! Where are you going?"

He didn't look back. "Outside."

"Outside?"

"Yeah." He cleared his throat. "Jason and Christina'll be here any minute." He stomped off, stepping over Dr. Mendle's lifeless body as he made his way to the doorway.

"Is she okay?" Violet said as she popped up behind him.

Relief swept over him. The cuts on her face were gone, so he assumed the rest of her was healing as well. It took all his strength not to kiss her and crush her to him. "Yeah," he glanced over at Georgina, who was rocking Grayson back and forth and soothing him.

"Oh my," she gasped. "Was that the child we heard?"

He nodded tersely, the memory of Grayson's scream sending ice through his veins. "We should get out of here. Luke's outside waiting for Jason and Christina." He turned to face her. "How are you?"

"All healed up."

"Violet." His voice was shaky as he brushed a lock of hair aside from her cheek. "I thought I almost lost you."

"What—" A gasp escaped her throat, and her eyes rolled back.

"Violet?"

Her eyes shut and her arms went limp. Nathan quickly caught her.

"Violet!" He picked her up and pushed her hair out of her face. "Baby, what's wrong?" His heart pounded against his rib cage as she remained unresponsive. "Violet say something!" Her skin was suddenly hot, spiking up a few degrees. Looking over to where she had stumbled back, he saw various liquids pooling on the floor around the broken glass. "Fuck!"

"What's wrong?" Georgina said as she came up to him, little Grayson still clutched to her.

"What was in those vials?"

Georgina bit her lip. "I ... I don't know. Dr. Mendle is so paranoid. He doesn't work with anyone or even have any lab assistants. I'm the only one here, but I do mostly menial cleanup."

Violet's body convulsed, but her eyes remained closed. "Shit! Fuck! Hang on, Baby. Please hang on. Let's go."

Nathan led them out of the lab and the facility, keeping

Violet close to him. *Please be okay, please be ok*, he repeated like a prayer.

"Nathan!" Christina ran toward them. "Nathan! What's going on? What happened?"

"I'll explain later." He nodded to Violet. "She's hurt. Or sick. I don't know what's wrong! But we need to get her to the hospital now."

"The car's this way." She looked behind her. "Jason! We gotta go now!"

They ran to the front of the factory where Jason's Range Rover was waiting. Nathan darted to the vehicle and opened the door, first letting Georgina and Grayson inside, then scooting in after them. He settled into the seat, keeping Violet close.

"You'll be okay, Baby," he whispered, kissing her forehead. Her skin was burning up bad.

Jason jumped into the driver's seat, and Christina sat in the front passenger side. "What's wrong with her?" she asked as Jason put the car into gear.

"A couple of vials fell on her. It could be poison," he said through gritted teeth.

Christina reached over and patted his knee. "We'll get her to Blackstone Hospital on time. Don't worry. She'll be okay." She turned to Georgina. "Are you okay, miss? Your neck is all red. Is he hurt?"

Georgina's lower lip trembled. "I'm f-f-ine. He's ... healed up." A whimper tore from her throat as tears gathered in her eyes.

Christina laid a hand on her knee. "It's okay ..."

"Georgina ..."

"I'm Christina, and this is my husband Jason," she said.

"And you're going to be fine. It's all over. You'll be safe from now on."

A sob escaped Georgina's lips, and she buried her face in Grayson's fine blond hair. Christina grabbed something from her purse—a handkerchief—and handed it to the other woman.

"I ... thank you ... I don't know what to say ..."

"Just relax. We'll be in Blackstone soon and you'll be safe."

"B-b-blackstone?"

"Yes. You were in Verona Mills."

"What state am I in?" she asked.

Nathan and Christina looked at each other. "Colorado," she said. "You didn't know?"

"I ..." Her voice choked.

"We can talk about this later," Christina said. "But just know you have nothing to worry about."

Violet let out a soft moan.

Nathan loosened his arms, unaware he'd been gripping her so tight. "Violet, say something, please."

"I ... Nathan ..." Her eyes flew open for a moment; her pupils were so dilated that her eyes were the color of coal. "So ... hot ... painful."

"Where does it hurt?"

"Everywhere," she gasped. When he put a hand on her cheek, her hand flew up and pressed it harder against her face. "Oh ... that feels good ... so better ...."

"Does that help, Baby?"

"Yes." She rubbed her nose against his palm. "Oh ..."

"Hang on," he said. "We're almost there."

They reached Blackstone Hospital in no time as Jason broke the speed limit all the way up to town. Christina had called ahead and as soon as they pulled into the entrance, the staff was there, ready with a gurney.

"We'll take it from here, sir," a nurse said as she gently pried Violet away from Nathan.

"No!" she protested. She had been semi-conscious and delirious throughout the whole ride. "I want to stay with you."

"It's all right, Violet," he said. "The nurses will take care of you." He didn't want to let her go, but there wasn't anything else he could do but trust the doctors would treat whatever was wrong with her.

Nathan kept his eyes on her as they placed her on the gurney and wheeled her off. Looking around, he saw someone was attending to Georgina and Grayson. His stomach clenched, and barely contained fury was bubbling inside him. He couldn't imagine what they'd been through if she didn't even know what city, much less state, she was being held in. Her husband or mate must be going mad by now; he knew he would be if it had been Violet and their cub who'd been kidnapped.

"Nathan?" Jason's voice broke through his thoughts. "You look terrible."

"Yeah? I feel awesome too," he joked.

Jason cracked a smile, his shoulders relaxing. "I'd ask you to go home and get some rest, but if I were in your place I wouldn't be able to."

"Thanks, man," he said.

"You, me, and Christina should go have a chat. It'll keep your mind occupied until the doctors are done, and you can tell us what happened while it's still fresh."

"Yeah well—fuck! Luke. And the other girls!" He'd been so worried out of his mind about Violet that he'd forgotten about them.

"No worries, man. When we arrived, Luke was putting the two girls in one of the cars parked inside the factory. Said he'd bring them here. I think I saw him leave just as we came."

"Good." He fished his phone out of his pocket. "I'm gonna give Melanie a call and then I'll meet you back here."

"So," Christina said as she took a sip of the terrible hospital coffee, "what you're saying is this group, whoever they are, established this lab just outside Blackstone to experiment on shifters? And the local government in Verona Mills is helping them cover up the kidnappings?"

"That's what the loony doctor said." Nathan wrinkled his nose at the paper cup, then tossed it into the wastebasket in the corner. The director of the hospital was kind enough to let them stay inside an empty conference room while they waited for news on Violet and Georgina.

Jason slammed his fist on the table. "Fuckers! I'm gonna burn every last one of them to ashes."

"We will find them and stop them." There was a steely determination in Christina's eyes. "At least now we know there really is an organization who's out to get us. They killed my mother and tried to blow us up during the wedding."

"And they tried to kidnap you," Jason reminded her. "So, this organization. Where do we start?"

"The lab," Christina said. "We need to go back and gather evidence." She cursed under her breath. "I just wish our office was already set up. We could have technicians and agents helping out."

"I don't care what it costs; we'll get The Agency up and

running in Blackstone within the week," Jason added. "That woman and her son. Georgina. What do we know about her?"

"She's still with the doctors," Christina said. "She could provide us with more information about the organization. We need to protect her and keep her close. If she knows anything, then they're going to want to find her before she talks."

"We'll give her whatever she needs," Jason said.

While they continued to discuss the next steps, a knock on the door made all three turn their heads. "Come in," Christina called.

The door opened and an older woman wearing a white coat stepped in. "Excuse me, Mr. Lennox. Mrs. Lennox. I'm Dr. Aurora Jenkins. I'm here about Dr. Robichaux's condition."

Nathan bolted up from his chair. "How is she? Is she okay?"

"Are you Mr. Nathan Caldwell?"

"I am," he said. "Is she asking for me?"

Dr. Jenkins hesitated. "She ... mentioned you by name, yes."

"Doc, please." Nathan stepped forward. "Tell us what happened."

"Sir, are you family?" she asked.

"No, but I'm her mate."

She sighed in relief. "Oh I see. That's why she asked for you when we explained the situation."

"What's wrong with her?" Christina asked.

Dr. Jenkins glanced at Christina and Jason. "I'm afraid it's a delicate private matter and something I should only discuss with Mr. Caldwell. We can go to her room so I can explain further."

"As long as she's going to be all right, we're good," Christina said.

Jason came up and clapped him on the back. "We'll be here. And doctor, whatever she needs, make sure she gets it no matter the cost."

"I will Mr. Lennox." She gestured to Nathan. "This way please, Mr. Caldwell."

Nathan followed the doctor out the conference room and down the hallway. His stomach was turning in nervousness, but Dr. Jenkins didn't seem to be in a hurry so maybe Violet's life wasn't in danger. He was, however, puzzled at why they couldn't discuss this in front of anyone else.

Dr. Jenkins opened the door to room 156 and gestured for Nathan to go in. He expected to see Violet, but it looked more like a meeting room. The doctor walked over to the window and raised the blinds. To his surprise, it wasn't a window to the outside but a view into another room.

"Violet!" He slammed his palms on the glass. Violet was lying on a hospital bed. Her eyes were closed, but she was moaning and twisting about. He spied the restraints on her ankles and wrists.

"What did you do to her?" he raged at Dr. Jenkins.

"Mr. Caldwell, I'm trying to explain," she said calmly. "Dr. Robichaux needs your help."

He looked back at Violet, his heart aching as he watched her. "I'll do anything. Now tell me what happened."

"There's no delicate way to do this so I'll come out and just say it. Dr. Robichaux was doused with some type of chemical that triggered her heat cycle."

"Excuse me?"

"Mature female feline shifters, as you know, have heat

cycles that come about twice a year. Whatever she came in contact with sent her body into a cycle."

"She's in ... heat?"

Dr. Jenkins took off her glasses, then massaged the bridge of her nose. "Yes. The chemical not only brought it on but intensified the symptoms. Not only is she ... sensitive all over, but she is in a lot of pain."

"What medicine are you giving her?"

"I can give her a mild sedative, but she'll burn it off a few minutes. I'm afraid, er, giving her relief is the only way to help her."

"Relief?"

"Sexual relief."

Oh. He swallowed hard.

"We had to put her in an isolation room to quarantine her," Dr. Jenkins warned. "With the pheromones she's giving off, we had to restrain a few of the male nurses when they scented her. I've cleared all non-female staff from the floor."

He clenched his jaw tight. "Thank you." He cleared his throat. "Is her life in danger?"

"Maybe. Maybe not. Her temperature is spiking to alarming levels. We could put her in a cold bath, but that won't lessen the pain."

Violet moaned and turned her body to the side, straining against the shackles. Her eyes went wide as she looked straight toward them. "Nathan," she whispered.

Nathan pressed his hands up to the glass. "Violet! Baby, I'm here! I'm going to take care of you, okay?"

"Nathan ... please ..." She reached out and then fell back on the bed.

He turned to Dr. Jenkins. "How long before this goes away?"

"I estimate it could be twenty-four hours at least, but most heat cycles don't last more than two days."

"Two days?" Fuck. He couldn't let her suffer like this. But what Dr. Jenkins was saying he had to do ... he didn't want to be with her like this. When he saw her hurt, he already knew he was going to make it up to her. But this ...

"Doc, I'm her mate but ... we haven't ... we're not at that stage in our relationship yet."

"Oh," Dr. Jenkins said. "I understand. You don't have to have full intercourse with her. Just keep her satisfied in other ways until the heat cycle runs its course. Even skin to skin contact seems to help. Also, there's a shop in town that could provide you with some aids—"

"Okay, Doc, I get it." He balled his hands into fists. He just had to keep giving her orgasms for a few hours. He supposed he could do that. But there was another problem. "Will she be conscious enough to give me consent?"

She seemed surprised by the question. "I assure you she's very lucid, Mr. Caldwell. She was able to tell us everything, her name, her job, what occurred before she arrived at the hospital. Dr. Robichaux knows what's happening to her. She asked to be restrained, in case the drugs made her lose control. And she asked for you specifically."

Nathan felt the blood pounding in his temples. Violet asked for him? To help her? "I need to get her out of here. I can take her to my apartment."

"She's overly sensitive right now. I can inject her with a pain reliever. It'll last for under an hour. But I have to warn you, when you come in contact with her, she'll be, uh, extremely friendly."

"That should be enough time." He grabbed the doorknob to the sealed room. "I'll take it from here, if you don't mind."

CHAPTER TWELVE

DR. JENKINS and two female nurses helped Nathan get Violet ready for the trip back to his place. They gave her the pain reliever and wrapped her up in a blanket, then brought her to the rear exit where he was waiting in Jason's Range Rover. He quickly explained to Jason and Christina what was happening, and they offered to help any way they could.

He was glad for the assistance because the moment he opened the door, Violet's scent hit him with such force his knees buckled. His cock went instantly hard, and he had to grab onto the bed to stop himself from taking her right then and there.

Nathan drove as quick as he could, keeping watch on the time. Once in a while, he would glance at the back seat to make sure Violet was okay. She was sleeping peacefully now, as they gave her a mild sedative as well. Her face was calm, and he took some comfort in knowing she wasn't in pain.

"We're almost there, Baby. Hang on." He pulled into his parking space and cut the engine. Taking Violet in his arms, he brought her up to his loft apartment using the stairs instead of the elevators, since he didn't want to run into any of his neighbors.

He unlocked the door with one free hand and walked inside, then reached behind him to put the deadbolt in place. He brought her up to his bedroom, laying her down gently on the king-sized bed.

Violet's skin was hot, even for a shifter. He quickly unwrapped the blankets from her body. Her scent filled his nostrils again, and he gripped the sheets tight in his fists.

Her eyes flew open, and when she saw him, her face broke into a weak smile. "Nathan," she said.

"Violet. How are you feeling?"

"Hot ... and so sensitive."

"Does it hurt?"

She grabbed his hand and pressed it against her cheek. "Not so much now."

He sucked in a breath. His body was ready; it wanted her so bad it was almost painful. But his mind ... "Violet, you know what's happening to you, right?"

She nodded, then moved his hand lower. Over her jaw, down her neck, to her breasts. A nipple pebbled under his fingers as soon as he grazed it. "Yes, I know. Nathan, I need you so bad," she mewled.

Fuck, she wasn't making this easy. And his body wasn't making this easy. Why was it hard to do the right thing? "Violet, baby, you know I want you too, right?"

"You do?"

"What I said to Ben? I was just saying it to get him off my back. Because ... because I couldn't believe someone beautiful and smart and classy like you could be mine."

"Nathan ... no—"

"Shhh ... it's okay. I just ... I want you, but not like this."

"But Nathan, I want you too. I want you inside of me. Fucking me."

Damn, he could have come right then and there hearing those words from her mouth. "Don't worry. The doc said I just need to keep you supplied with orgasms until your heat runs out. I can do that. But the rest ... let's wait until we can talk about us, okay? And clear the air?"

Her plump lips parted. "But what about you? Don't you want to feel good too?"

"Just watching you come is good enough for me," he said. "Can I help you out, Violet? Take away your pain?"

She nodded. "Yes. Please Nathan. Touch me."

Nathan made quick work of the paper-thin hospital gown, using his claws to quickly tear it away from her body. She was completely naked underneath.

"God, you're gorgeous."

Perfectly round and perky breasts. Pink nipples. Smooth skin all over. A neatly trimmed landing strip over her mound. And her scent. It was even stronger now, like he was drowning in honey. He leaned down and captured a nipple in his mouth, his tongue teasing the bud. His other hand went to the other breast, cupping it and brushing the tip with his fingers. When his teeth accidentally grazed her, her body shook and she moaned his name out loud, her fists curling into the sheets underneath them.

"Fuck," he said as he popped the nipple out of his mouth. He could feel her skin cool down slightly. "Violet, did you just ..."

"Uh-huh." She looked down and smiled at him. "And the pain is gone."

He breathed a sigh of relief. "Thank God." He collapsed on

the bed beside her and closed his eyes. Maybe this wouldn't be so hard.

"Nathan," she purred. He felt her move, swing a leg over him, and climb on top. She ran her hands down his chest, then grabbed the bottom of his shirt.

The sound of fabric ripping made him open his eyes. Violet had torn his shirt to shreds and was running her fingers down his chest.

"You're so sexy," she said. "God, it's like these were painted on." Her hands slid over his abs, then lower to his jeans.

Fuck, she was really making this hard. And making something else harder as she ground her hips over the bulge between his legs. He shouldn't have looked down, but he couldn't stop himself. Her pussy lips were glistening as she rubbed them on the denim of his jeans.

"Baby," he said, carefully rolling her onto her back again. He covered her with his body, pinning her down. Her skin was warming up again. "You still feel okay?"

"Uh-huh. I just want to make you feel good too."

"You do." He skimmed his fingers down over her belly to her mound. He skipped over her clit for now and rubbed his digits over her slick cunt lips. "So wet. Do you want to come again?"

"Yes! Please make me come." She was thrusting her hips up at him.

"Don't worry, Baby, I'll keep you coming." He teased her at first, making her breath come in soft pants and sighs. When he sank one finger to her wet, hot heat, she cried out and lifted her body off the bed. His thumb found her clit, and the moment he touched it, her pussy flooded his fingers with her wetness.

"More," she moaned. "Please."

He thrust another finger inside her, moving his hand back and forth. Gritting his teeth, he tried to ignore the pain in his cock as he stroked her to another orgasm. Her sweet, tight pussy clenched at his fingers, her pert little ass lifting off the bed as she came.

He didn't think he could want her more, but her scent was intoxicating. And he had to have a taste. Pressing her back down onto the mattress, he spread her knees and moved between her thighs.

God, he never thought he'd see heaven, but this had to be close. Her warm thighs around his head and her soft pink pussy against his mouth. She cried out when his lips touched her, her fingers raking against his scalp in a way that made him shiver. Her sweet honey flowed into his mouth, firing off synapses in his brain he never knew existed.

"Nathan, oh God! I'm coming!"

He worked her pussy harder, coaxing the orgasm from her body, licking at her and thrusting his tongue into her while his thumb stroked her clit. His efforts were rewarded as her hips convulsed, and her fingernails left marks on his shoulders as her orgasm tore through her.

"Nathan," she sighed as she sank down into the mattress. "Oh. That was good."

"Just good?" he teased.

She chuckled. "Excellent. Amazing ..."

"But?"

"But," she looked down at him with a pout, "you haven't kissed me yet."

He grinned and crawled over her body. "You want to taste yourself?" When she nodded, he lowered his lips to hers, their tongues touching in an erotic dance. He sighed against her mouth, then pulled away.

"Feeling better?"

She nodded. "I think I'll be okay for a bit." A pink flush bloomed over her cheeks. Violet was actually blushing but not from the heat. He thought it was the most adorable thing. "You can rest if you want." He gave her a quick kiss on the lips. "Be right back." Hopping off the bed, he walked to his bathroom in the corner, then closed the door behind him.

Nathan braced himself on the sink, took a deep breath, and looked up into the mirror. *You're doing this for her*, he told himself. His conscience was the only thing keeping him from sliding his cock into her sweet cunt, and his control was wearing thin. *Maybe I can relieve myself for now.* Popping the buttons on his jeans, he eased them down along with his underwear, and wrapped a hand around his shaft. He grunted and began to stroke his length.

A gasp caught him by surprise. He didn't even hear the door open. "Violet, I—"

"It's okay," she said, walking toward him. She was naked; her hair fell around her shoulders and perfect tits, her pussy on display. "I should have known." She placed her hands on his chest.

His back hit the tile wall with a soft thud. Before he knew it, Violet was on her knees in front of him. Her small delicate hand wrapped around his cock. "You don't need to ..."

"I know," she said, looking up at him, her face centimeters from his cock. "But I want to."

"Vio—nngh!" His head slammed back against the wall the moment her lips closed around him. Jesus, her mouth was warm and wet, her rough tongue stroking him in all the right places. *Fuck. Jesus Fucking Christ.*

He thrust his fingers into her hair, slowing her down. She was eagerly sucking him off, but he didn't want to blow his load yet. He wanted to enjoy the feel of her mouth for just a bit longer.

"Violet," he moaned as he released her hair. Her head bobbed up and down vigorously, her lips wrapped around him. "Fuck. Shit, fucking fuck!" His vision turned white, and he swore he saw stars as his orgasm ripped through him. His cock convulsed, and Violet continued to pleasure him with her mouth, swallowing down every drop of his cum.

When his heartbeat slowed down and returned to normal, he let out a long breath. Violet stood up and wiped her mouth with the back of her hand. "Was that good?"

He laughed. "Baby, I don't have the words to describe it." He pulled her to him, letting her lay her cheek on his chest. She was starting to warm up again, and she was rubbing her nose against him. "How about a cool shower?" Dr. Jenkins had said it might help keep her body temperature down and ease some heat symptoms.

"That sounds wonderful," she said. "Join me?"

"Only if I get to soap you up."

CHAPTER THIRTEEN

VIOLET WOKE SLOWLY, her body feeling deliciously sore. She reached down, laying her palms over her stomach and moving them up to breasts and neck. Her skin temperature was normal now, and the pain was gone. The edges of her vision were clear, not blurred out. That constant ache between her legs wasn't there, either. She heaved a sigh of relief. This was why she took suppressants the first chance she could.

Her mother had prepared her for her first heat, of course, but there was no way she could have expected what it was like. It came when she was seventeen. She had to stay in her room and keep the door and windows sealed so she didn't attract any non-related males in the area. And she had to relieve the ache by touching herself and using toys constantly. Her first heat had only lasted twelve hours, thank God, but she told her mother she would be taking suppressants and birth control from that moment on until she was ready for cubs. She couldn't imagine being out in the field and having that inconvenience thrust upon her.

Her tiger let out a happy purr and laid down in a contented manner. *Mine.*

She glanced over at Nathan's muscled back. Did the chemical that induced her heat make her lose her mind and ask for him? Maybe. But she supposed she should be grateful he was there. The pain was nearly unbearable, and her fever was getting to dangerous levels. It wasn't as bad when Nathan was carrying and touching her, so she knew he would be able to help. Besides, what was she supposed to do? Ask for male volunteers in town? She and Nathan were compatible. It seemed like the logical solution. Yes, that was it. It had nothing to do with the fact that she'd been wanting to know how hard those abs of his were. And what his skin tasted like—

"Huh!"

Nathan sat up quickly, and Violet pulled her hand away. She didn't even realize she'd been stroking his back.

"Sorry," she said, scooting away to the edge of the bed. "I didn't mean ..."

He turned around, and as soon as he saw her, his wicked mouth spread into a smile. "Good morning, gorgeous." He crawled over to her and gathered her into his arms, then placed his chin on top her head. "How are you this morning?"

"Better," she murmured against his chest. Oh, he smelled so good. And felt so good. There was a tingling between her legs again, and it had nothing to do with her estrus cycle. It reminded her they hadn't yet had sex. He was so thoughtful, but it really was unnecessary. She had given him full consent, but he had been adamant about not having intercourse. They had done everything *but*, so why stop now? And her heat cycle had passed, so he couldn't have any more objections.

"Violet?"

"Hmmm?" She was rubbing his thigh, moving her hand up slowly until she came to his cock. Fully erect already. Her previous partners had all been human, but she had heard that male shifters had an excellent refractory period. Nathan was probably even more of an outlier. Not only was he able to recover quickly, but his repeat performances were quite astounding.

"What are you doing?" he asked in a low voice.

Her hand wrapped around him. "What do you think?"

"Are you still in pain?" he asked quickly. "Do you need me to help you?"

"Oh no." She lay down and pulled him on top of her. "Nathan, my estrus cycle has taken its full course. I'm once again of sound mind and body, but let me remind you I was fully conscious of what was going on last night."

The press of his body on top of her was delicious, and he groaned as his thick shaft rubbed against her. She herself was fully aroused and could feel the wetness between her legs.

"Baby ... you make it so hard ..."

"Oh good. That's the idea." She pushed her hips toward him, the underside of his cock sliding against her slick lips.

"No, I mean, you make it hard to do the right thing."

"Nathan, you saved me from a lot of pain ... or worse. I want to do this. Please." She arched her back. "I need you inside me."

He bit out a curse. "Violet ..."

"We've had about twenty-hours of foreplay. I think I've had enough."

He grit his teeth and pressed his forehead to hers. "If you're sure."

"I am." She stared up into his depthless green eyes. "Are you?"

"I've never been so fucking sure of anything else."

Violet closed her eyes as he moved a hand between them. She felt the tip of his cock nudge at her and slowly enter. She sucked in a breath as he filled her, pushing in all the way. She'd never felt so full in her life.

"Violet." Nathan's callused fingers stroked at her temple. "Baby." His lips caressed hers, moving against her mouth in a sensual kiss. His tongue licked at her, coaxing her open, and she could only comply.

He began to move his hips, pulling back and pushing in again. Each thrust sent zings of pleasure through her body, all the way down to make her toes curl. She raked her nails down his back and his buttocks, digging her fingers into his taut skin to urge him to go faster.

"Baby," he whispered. "So good ... so tight."

"Keep going," she urged. "I'm almost ... ah!"

"Fuck. Fuck. Fuck." He scooped his hands under her, pushing her up so he could thrust deeper and harder into her. She wrapped her legs around him and clung to his shoulders as he pummeled into her. "God ... I—"

"Nathan!" The orgasm rocked her body, coming so quickly she didn't anticipate it. Surprise made her sink her teeth into his shoulder, which in turn made him growl and thrust harder into her. She felt him spasm and throb inside her as she gripped him harder. His whole body stiffened, and he grunted as he pushed deep into her. He called out her name and then relaxed, laying his body gently down over hers.

Violet thought that maybe she passed out. She had closed her eyes, and her body felt limp as she lost all thought. When she opened them, they were still in the same position. Nathan's skin was damp on hers, and his breathing slowed to a normal pace.

"Violet," he whispered. "You're doing it again."

"Huh?" The vibrations in her chest were louder. She was purring. "Oh … I've never done that before. With anyone else, I mean."

"So … your tiger…."

"Oh." When she saw those men yesterday, with their guns, her tiger just ripped out of her. It wasn't exactly her intention to show herself to Nathan that way. "You've never heard of a golden tiger before?"

"No. Is that a breed?"

"It's a genetic mutation," she said. "Both my parents apparently had the recessive gene, so I had a higher chance of receiving it."

"It's beautiful."

"Really?" No one had ever said that. She always hated the way her stripes were uneven and how her fur was shaggy and soft. Plus, she was larger than most tiger shifters.

"You really are my beautiful mutant." His eyes lit up. "And you're cute when you blush."

"I do not blush!" she denied, even though she felt the heat on her cheeks.

"You're doing it now, too."

When she tried to wiggle away from him, he rolled them over so she was on top. His strong arms clamped around her to keep her in place. "Nathan."

He groaned as he slipped out of her, his cum leaking down her thighs.

"I should—" She tried to push off him, but he held her tighter instead.

"Yes?"

The smile he gave her was so boyish and naughty, she

couldn't help but grin back. She brushed a lock of hair away from his forehead. "Are you okay?"

He laughed. "Shouldn't I be asking *you* that?"

"I'm feeling fine," she said.

"Just fine? Then I did something wrong. We should try again—"

"Nathan!" She playfully swatted him on the shoulder. "I'm more than fine. I told you, the cycle has passed."

"And the sex?"

"Hmmm, that was something," she said with a sigh and laid her head on his chest.

"What something?"

She placed her chin on his chest and raised a brow. "Are you fishing for compliments, Mr. Caldwell?"

"Were you thinking of giving them out, Dr. Robichaux?" he asked with a cheeky grin.

"Well—"

A vibrating sound made them both turn their heads. Nathan sighed and reached for his phone. "I haven't spoken to anyone since yesterday."

"Go ahead," she said, rolling off him. "I'll get cleaned up."

Violet went into the bathroom to freshen up. When she walked out, Nathan was nodding and talking softly into the phone.

"Good. Thanks for letting me know. Bye."

"Everything ok—" She gasped, realizing that after she collapsed she had no idea what happened. "Oh no."

"Baby?" He rushed to her side. "What's the matter?"

"Joanne. The girl. Georgina! And her son?" She sank down on the bed. "I didn't even think—"

"Shhh, Violet." He put an arm around and pulled her to his side. "It's all right. They're safe. All of them. I called Melanie as soon as we got to the hospital. Luke brought Joanne and the other girl to the hospital, and they're fine too. Georgina and her son, Grayson, came with us. They're safe." He frowned.

"What's wrong?"

"That was Jason. He and Christina went back to the lab. It was burned to the ground when they got there."

She gasped. "Oh no."

"Yeah. But we're not going to let them get away with what they did."

"Good." She stood up, but Nathan grabbed her hand and pulled her onto his lap. "Nathan, we need to—"

"We don't have to do anything right now," he whispered against her neck. "I also told Jason you were still indisposed. That we needed another day or two for you to recover."

"But what about work? I'm perfectly—oh!" His teeth nipped at her lobe. "Uhm, perhaps I could use some time to rest."

Nathan pulled her down and laid her flat on her back. "You definitely still look sick," he said, his lips on her breast.

"Then I should stay in bed to ... recover."

CHAPTER FOURTEEN

VIOLET WOULD HAVE BEEN PERFECTLY happy to spend the rest of the week in bed. Nathan was a skilled lover, and the pleasure he gave her was unlike anything she'd experienced before. But she knew they had to come out of his apartment sometime, so the next day she insisted he drive her back to her hotel so she could change clothes and they could go back to work.

He tried to tempt her into taking off another day. If she gave in, they might never make it out of his place. Nathan sulked, but he didn't stay too mad, not when she coaxed him into a quickie before they drove off to work.

She kept busy at the mines, collecting samples and analyzing the results from the previous tests. Since she'd missed two days of collections, she'd have to work double time to make up for it. Plus, she had to go through the stack of resumes that had piled up in her inbox.

A knot tightened in her stomach. Had she really been so distracted that she had forgotten about her agreement with

Ben? And about Antonia and the girls? She hadn't heard back from Antonia for a while, nor from the non-profit agency she'd been negotiating with to secure funding.

Before she was forced to leave, she promised Antonia she would find a way to get them out of the village. She was going to bring them down to the nearby town and help them establish a formal orphanage where the girls could be safe and attend school. She used every connection she had and hopped to Switzerland and France, then finally to London where she had a meeting with a non-profit that seemed fruitful. Girl's Liberty Trust, or GLT, focused on helping women and children in war zones. They looked over her proposal and told her they would get back to her, but they were positive they could approve the funding. She felt somewhat relieved but knew it was not over yet. She took the next flight back to the States so she could do her interview in Blackstone.

"Everything okay, Baby?"

She nearly jumped out of her seat when she heard Nathan's voice. He was standing in the doorway of their office.

"Yes, I'm fine. Just thinking." The knot in her stomach grew bigger, and her heart felt heavy. He knew about the girls. Surely if the funding came through and she had to leave, he would understand, right? They had made no promises to each other. In any case, it could still be months before she got the money. They could be tired of each other by then and perhaps their relationship, if she could call it that, would fizzle out naturally like her other liaisons.

Her tiger let out an angry hiss at the thought. *Mine.*

She pushed the word down deep inside her along with her tiger. She thought the damn thing would be satisfied by now. It was practically glowing the past two days, especially around

Nathan. The tiger was especially happy knowing he thought it was *beautiful*.

"Are you sure you're okay?" Nathan walked closer to her.

"These test results are riveting," she lied, pointing to the screen. "Did you know that blackstone is about twenty times harder than diamonds?"

He hauled her to her feet and then pulled her to him. "I can think of something that's getting hard right now." He gave her a wink before leaning down to kiss her.

"Eww! Gross!"

They broke apart and turned their heads toward the door.

"What are you doing here, Kate?" Nathan asked, his face setting into a scowl.

"Tsk, tsk, why aren't you in a better mood? Don't you know sex boosts endorphins?" She sauntered into the office, then leaned her hip against Violet's table. "Besides, I'm scheduled to check on the network today. Or did your sex-hazed brain forget that?"

Nathan crossed his arms over his chest. "Get what you need done, then leave."

"What? You're not happy to see your sister?" She stuck her tongue out at him, then looked at Violet. "Hey, Vi. I'd ask you how you're doing, but since you're banging my brother I'd rather not know."

"Er, was there something you needed from me?" Violet asked as she sat back down.

"Why, yes! I was hoping to run into you. We—that's me and all the girls—are having a baby shower for Penny this weekend." Kate hopped up and planted herself on top of the desk. "You should come."

"I'm not really sure … I mean, I don't know her very well. I'd be happy to send a gift."

"Pshaw. Don't worry; it's fine. A couple of other new people are coming. Georgina and her adorable little cub will be there."

"Oh." She did want to see how Georgina and Grayson were doing. "I suppose I could drop by."

"Great!" Kate hopped off the desk. "It's eleven a.m. at Rosie's. Wear something blue or pink, whichever you think the baby will be." She shook her head at Nathan. "Sorry, girls only."

Nathan rolled his eyes. "I'll be sad for a bit, but I'll get over it."

"Bye," Kate said. "Oh and Nathan? Make sure you call Mom and Dad soon." She looked meaningfully at Violet and winked at him. "Before I do."

"Just get out." Nathan walked to his sister and gently pushed her out the door. "Damn nosy Kate," he grumbled. "Sorry about that. I don't know how she knows."

"Knows what?"

"About us. I mean, you and me—"

"Having sex?"

"Yeah."

She shrugged. "Sex is a natural thing, you know."

He chuckled. "Yeah, but," he stalked back to her, "I was hoping to keep you to myself just for a little bit."

"Oh." His words made a thrill run down her spine, and she didn't know why. So she swiveled her chair back to her monitor. "I should get back to this."

"Violet." He pivoted her chair back around. "Is something the matter?"

She swallowed a gulp. "Nothing. Not at all."

CHAPTER FIFTEEN

NATHAN FROWNED as Violet mumbled an excuse and left the trailer. He didn't know why, but suddenly something had changed. Maybe she just needed some time to herself.

His wolf whined unhappily.

Jeez, buddy. She's not going to Africa, he admonished. But still, there was a creeping feeling in his chest he couldn't ignore. What could be wrong? Why did chicks act so weird sometimes?

A thought popped into his head. Weren't girls always talking about commitment and defining relationships and shit? Maybe that was why she was worked up today. He didn't know where they stood either, but he was pretty sure from now on she would be the only woman for him.

"That's it."

Violet wasn't feeling secure about them. They never did have that conversation before they had sex. She knew about his past, about all the women. Now, she only had to see that she was his only future.

He knew what he had to do. A grand gesture or some shit like that. To show her he was serious about her.

It took him all afternoon to think of a plan, but he figured it all out. He couldn't wait to tell Violet.

"Huh." He glanced up at the clock. She'd been gone for hours. Where could she be? He got up from his desk and walked out of the office. Her trace scent was in the air, and he followed his nose, leading him down to one part of the cave they still hadn't explored. Dr. Philipps had said it had the potential to be a particularly rich vein. *Of course that was where she'd be*, he thought with a smile. He kept walking until he saw a small figure looking up at the wall.

"Fascinating," she exclaimed as she looked up at a large chunk of blackstone stuck in the glittering *nitride londaleite*.

"Violet?"

She jumped at the sound of his voice, then turned around. "Nathan. Thank God it's you."

"Who else would it be?" he asked as he came closer. "Baby, it's nearly six p.m."

She blinked. "I didn't realize I was gone that long."

"Well, it's time to go. C'mon, let's go back to your hotel."

"Good idea," she said as they walked out of the cave system.

He grinned at her. "Glad you think so. I'll help you pack up and check out and then we can grab some burgers at the diner."

She stopped short. "Excuse me?"

"Or would you prefer pizza?"

Turning to face him, she put her hands on her hips. "What do you mean pack up and check out?"

"So you can come home with me," he said. "To our place."

"Our place?" she echoed.

"Yeah, my place. Our place. It's all the same now. Now come on—"

"I'm not moving into your loft."

He must have heard her wrong. "Of course you are. Let's go."

"How dare you!" She shrugged his hand off her.

"Violet." His voice turned low and serious. "You're my mate."

"No, I'm not. We haven't even experienced the mating bond."

"So? In time we will." He was sure of it. Jason had said he'd know it when it happened. "Violet, I'm trying to be romantic here."

"Romantic?" she scoffed. "How is this romantic? What makes you think I want to move in with you? I hardly know you."

Her words slashed at him and made his wolf whimper. How could she even say that? Sure, it had been less than a week since they met, but he knew who *she* was. His mate. A muscle ticked along his jaw.

"Nathan let's be practical." That cool expression settled on her face. "There's no reason for me to just pack up and live with you when I'll be leaving soon anyway."

Blood pounded in his temples. "Leaving?"

"I've been saying that since the beginning. I'm only here on a temporary basis. I have plans and—"

"Right." His voice turned cold. That's right; she wasn't going to stay in Blackstone. He'd been stupid to think she would change her mind just because they slept together.

"Nathan, you should know—"

He cut her off. "Of course. I understand. You do have bigger and better things to do than stay in this sad little town, right?" He remembered how it rankled him, the way she breezed into Blackstone and turned her nose up, telling everyone she was only here temporarily and rubbing it in his face that she was leaving soon.

"I *never* called it sad," she protested. "But I can't stay here."

His wolf begged him to make her change her mind, but his bruised ego wouldn't let him. "I wish you well then." He pivoted and turned around.

"Nathan! Wait! Can we—"

"I'll see you tomorrow." He didn't want to hear what she had to say. Not when the pain in his chest was making him want to tear up everything in sight.

After what they'd been through, he thought things would be different. He had thought Violet put up a frosty mask to hide her hurt and trauma. But no; he was wrong. It was the complete opposite. *It wasn't a mask.*

She really was an unfeeling bitch.

CHAPTER SIXTEEN

VIOLET WATCHED NATHAN WALK AWAY, her throat burning and the air squeezing out of her lungs. Her tiger slashed at her insides, raging with pain and hurt.

"Stop," she hissed. "Get it together. We need to be strong. For the girls." She pictured their little faces, happy and laughing, and Nadia's shy gap-toothed grin.

It was just as she'd thought. This whole mate thing was a distraction. A derailment from her real goals. How dare he, anyway? What the hell made him think he could just control her like that? Like she was some doll he could move around and play with as he pleased. Moving in was a big leap even if they were already sleeping together. He couldn't just tell her they were going to start living together like it was a fact.

She took those feelings and put them away for now. Balling her hands into fists, she vowed to get things rolling with the funding. She would follow up with GLT in London as soon as she got to her hotel, and if they didn't have any positive news, then she'd have to find another way.

As it turns out, she didn't even have to call them. The moment she got in, there was already a message waiting for her from Lydia MacPhearson, the coordinator at GLT. She scribbled down the number in the message and immediately called her back.

"Lydia, it's Dr. Violet Robichaux."

"Oh, Dr. Robichaux," Lydia greeted in her Scottish brogue. "Thanks for calling back so fast."

"Of course. What news do you have?"

Lydia's voice turned serious. "I have good news and bad news. Your funding came through."

Relief washed over her. "Thank God. But what's the bad news?"

"Well …" Violet could hear Lydia chewing her lip. "I'm afraid Marcus, our field coordinator in Eritana who went to confirm your case, had an update for us."

"What did he say?"

"The villagers are forcing Antonia and her orphanage off the mountains. They want them gone soon."

Her tiger's claws came out. "But she never said anything or even called me."

"You gave her your phone, correct? Marcus said someone had stolen it."

Violet sank down on the bed. "Oh no. How are they?"

"According to Marcus' last check in with us, they're fine but scared. They can't even go out of the orphanage for fear of retaliation. The villagers are saying they brought the 'Golden Demon' into their midst, whatever that means, so now they have to leave."

Pure, white hot rage coursed through her veins. Her tiger roared with fury. They would see what the Golden Demon would could really do. "I'll head there as soon as I can."

"You don't have to; there's not much you can do until we have the funds released. That could still take up to two weeks."

"I'll be there." Her voice was determined. "I'll coordinate with you as soon as I'm on the ground." She hung up before Lydia could protest.

Her stomach clenched thinking about Antonia and the girls. She thought she'd warned off the rebels from trying to take them, but soon they'd be vulnerable again. She had to get to them, protect them in any way she could. But she wasn't sure how. After spending her entire savings to fly around Europe, there wasn't much left over. Her parents could help but that would mean answering a lot of questions, including why she'd quit her dream job.

She glanced at the stack of resumes she'd brought home. The agreement. If she could produce some good candidates, Lennox Corp. was going to give her that big bonus Ben promised. With that money, she could keep Antonia and the girls safe now.

Her thoughts drifted to Nathan, and a vice-like grip tightened around her chest. She grabbed the first resume off the pile, her hastiness sending the rest flying to the ground.

"Goddamnit!"

Never mind. There were many in her field who would be eager to study blackstone, so it shouldn't be hard to find a replacement. She'd start with this first candidate and see where that would lead.

———

The next day, Violet marched into Ben's office with four folders. The bear shifter look startled as she tossed them onto his desk.

"Good morning," he said.

"Here are four excellent candidates. One of them is within driving distance and would be more than happy to be here by this afternoon and start by Monday," she said.

Ben looked at the folders, then back to Violet. "Come again?"

Violet huffed. "I've found your candidates, so I'm leaving now. I trust that HR can process my bonus by next week."

His blond brows furrowed together. "Is there something you want to talk about?"

"There's nothing to discuss. I've completed the terms of our agreement, so I can leave now. I've already booked my flight to leave tomorrow afternoon."

"Tomorrow?" Ben said in an incredulous voice. "Violet, you can't—"

"It's done," she said, the words were making her heart grow heavy. "Go ahead and sue me if you want, but I read every word of my contract and I know I'm within my rights."

He heaved a sigh. "I'm not going to sue you, Violet. Could we please talk about this? Have a seat."

"I'll keep standing."

"Violet, sit down, please."

"No, thank you."

"Sit *down*. Please."

Her tiger shrank back at the sound of his voice and dominant power of Ben's bear. That was obviously not a request. She planted herself on the chair.

"Thank you," Ben said. "So you're leaving Blackstone. What does Nathan have to say about this?"

"What does he have to do with this?"

Ben rubbed a hand down his face. "I thought you were ... Jason told me you were together. As mates."

"We're not," she said. "Nor were we ever. While we may have slept together, it didn't mean anything." The words rang hollow in her ears.

"What?" The shock was evident in his face and voice. "That's not ... that can't ..."

"It's true," she said. "You can ask him yourself. He was the one who walked away from me yesterday." Technically true. He didn't want to hear her explanation at all. A small part of her wanted to believe he would understand.

"I'm ... sorry. And surprised." He heaved a long sigh. "I guess I have nothing else to say except good luck in your future plans."

"Thank you." She swallowed the burning tears in her throat as she stood up.

"Wait," he said. "What time's your flight?"

"Five-thirty." Why would he need to know? "I'll be returning my rental car to Verona Mills airport so I won't need a ride."

"Oh good. But I asked because Penny's baby shower is tomorrow."

She had forgotten about that. "I'll send a gift, I promise."

"No, it's not that. She's been really looking forward to it, you know? And she's had these mood swings, with the hormones and things." He scratched the back of his head. "It would be really nice if you stopped by, even for a sec. For me, too," he said sheepishly. "If you left without saying goodbye, she'll be bawling and crying and probably blame me like she does with everything these days."

She had heard pregnancy hormones made some women overly emotional. "Well, I suppose—"

"You'd be doing me a real big favor. I'll return it and make sure you get the bonus by Monday. Tuesday, tops."

"All right then." Penny and the other girls had been kind to her during the picnic. She at least owed them a farewell. "I'll be there."

CHAPTER SEVENTEEN

IT WAS easy enough to pack up her hotel room. Violet didn't have a lot of clothes in the first place, and most of them were still in her suitcase. Had the picnic only been a week ago? It seemed hard to believe. Seven days ago she was at the lake laughing with Kate, Penny, and Sybil, enjoying the water and then Nathan—

An involuntary shiver rushed through her body, and she took the feelings and memories and locked them away again. She would not think of Nathan. Not now. Not ever.

She stood outside Rosie's Bakery and Café, holding a brightly colored gift box in her hand. A feeling of dread washed over her, and she wasn't sure why. This was a happy day, right? She would be off to London and then connect on to Eritana. By Tuesday morning, she'd be on her way up the mountains to see the girls.

Scrounging up every bit of courage she had, Violet pushed through the doors and walked inside. The smell of delicious pastry and butter and sugar tickled her nose.

"Are you here for Penny's baby shower?" An older lady wearing a '50s-style blue dress asked her. Her name tag read "Rosie."

"Yes," she said.

Rosie nodded to the corner booth where a group of nearly a dozen women were gathered. "Head over there, honey. Everyone's here."

"Thank you," she said and made her way to the women.

The shower had taken up three booths, and there was a table laden with gifts. Penny was seated in the middle booth, her face bright as she laughed at something Kate said.

"Vi! You made it!" Kate dashed to her side. She took the gift from her hands and placed it on the table.

"Thank you for inviting me," she said with a tight smile. "I can't stay very long."

"Of course you can," Kate insisted, tugging her along. "Everyone this is Violet Robichaux. Vi, you know Penny, Sybil, Christina, and Catherine." She nodded to the pretty blonde woman next to Penny. "That's Amelia, she's Ben's sister. That's Dutchy; she's fabulous." The petite redhead next to Christina laughed. "Oh, and you know Georgina, right?"

Violet looked to the brunette sitting next to Catherine with the small boy in her lap. Georgina looked up at her warmly, then got to her feet, placing the boy at her hip.

"It's you!" she said in an excited voice. "We haven't met formally. I'm Georgina Mills, and this is my son, Grayson. Thank you for saving us." Her voice choked up as she embraced Violet.

"Uh, you're welcome." She hugged the woman back, then pulled away. "I'm glad you and your son are safe. Will you be going home to your husband soon?" She smiled at the little boy who was the spitting image of his mother except for the reddish blond hair. "I'm sure Grayson is missing his dad."

Before she could answer, Grayson said, "My daddy's in heaven. He went there while I was in mommy's tummy."

Georgina's lips thinned into a tight smile. "Grayson …"

"They're staying with us for a while," Catherine explained quickly. "You like living in the castle, don't you Grayson?"

The little boy's face lit up. "Oh boy, yeah! I've got toys and books and Ms. Meg makes the best chocolate chip cookies. And the castle is cool! Ms. Catherine said she'd come exploring with me some time, and Mr. Jason's gonna give me a ride on his back."

"That sounds lovely." If there was one thing Violet didn't regret about coming to Blackstone was that Georgina and Grayson were safe. The little boy seemed happy despite of what happened to him.

Kate introduced her to the rest of the women, who were mostly Penny's human co-workers from The Den. "Have some pie. It's amazing," Kate said, pulling Violet down to sit next to her.

"I'm not hungry, thank you."

Ignoring her, Kate put a plate in front of Violet. "Now, you missed the first game, but don't worry. We have plenty more."

Sybil snorted. "We are *not* doing the one where we sniff what's in the diaper. Knowing you we'd find more than just melted candy bars."

Kate waved at her. "Pshaw, it'll be fun." She frowned at Violet. "Why are you wearing black? I said wear pink or blue, right?"

Violet looked down at her blouse. It was the last clean shirt she had. "I didn't have anything in either color. And I told you, I wasn't planning on staying too long."

"Ugh, that brother of mine sucks! He can't keep you to himself all the time, you know!" She took her phone out of her pocket. "I'm going call him now and give him a piece of my—"

"NO!" Violet smacked Kate's hand, sending her phone skidding across the bright red Formica table.

The room went silent and several pairs of eyes turned to her.

Damn.

Violet slung the strap of her purse over her shoulder, then began to slide out of the booth. "I should—"

But Sybil was too fast, and she sat in the empty space beside her, blocking her way. "What's going on, Violet?"

"Nothing," she bit out. She turned to Penny. "Congratulations. I wish you and your cub well. If you'll excuse me, I don't want to be late for my flight."

"Flight?" Penny chewed on her lower lip. "You're leaving Blackstone?"

"Why?" Kate asked. "What about Nathan?"

"What about him?"

"He's your mate," Sybil stated.

"What did he do?" Kate pushed her imaginary sleeves to her elbows. "I swear to God I'll kick his ass!"

"Are you sure—"

"But why—"

"You guys need to—"

"You can't leave, Violet—" Sybil said.

Violet slammed her hands on the table. "Stop! Please!" Her heart sank when she looked at their stunned faces. "I can't … I have to leave. I can't stay here." She swallowed the tears burning in her throat.

"Why?" Christina asked.

"It's a matter of life and death." She took a deep breath and gave them a quick explanation of what happened in Eritana and what had transpired between her and Nathan.

"Nathan's such an asshole," Amelia said, rolling her eyes. "Men. They think they can control us. Ugh."

"So wait," Kate said. "My brother asked you to move in with him, found out you wanted to leave to build a freakin' orphanage, then broke up with you? He's going to be *so* dead!"

"Uh, not exactly," Violet said. "I didn't tell him I was going back to Eritana. I just said I was leaving."

"Violet," Catherine began. "That information seems kind of vital."

Violet blinked. "Why? Does it matter? He knew from the beginning I was leaving."

"Yes, but maybe this is all a misunderstanding," Sybil said. "You need to talk to him."

"He was the one who walked away from me," she said, her voice raising. "We could have easily sat down and talked about it like adults, but his damn ego wouldn't let him." She stood up. "Did I want to live with him? Of course I did! But he didn't have to bulldoze his way into it; he could have asked me! Besides, what were we going to do when I had to leave? I had no choice, but he did. Was he going to fly halfway around the world, leave his family and his job, to live in the middle of nowhere? I couldn't take his whole life away from him! I love —" She stopped, her hand going to her mouth. "I have to go."

Sybil seemed too stunned to stop her and didn't protest when Violet pushed her out of the booth so she could leave. She thought she heard the other women calling her, but the roaring blood in her ears drowned out them and everything else around her.

She bolted toward her parked car, opened the door, and

put the key in the ignition. The engine roared to life, but her hand froze on the gear shift.

What she almost said back there ... She was glad she stopped herself in time before she said it out loud. Because if she didn't say it, it wasn't true, right?

Placing the car in gear, she eased out of her spot. No, it was better this way. She had twenty-two girls counting on her, and she couldn't let them down. In time, the stabbing pain in her gut and heart would go away. She'd put those feelings aside and bury them as deep as she could so she would never feel this way again.

CHAPTER EIGHTEEN

"MOTHERFUCKING SHIT ASSHOLE!" Nathan wiped the sweat from his brow and kicked the toolbox by his foot. With a deep sigh, he stepped back from the weight belt feeder and grabbed a dirty rag from the table, wiping the grease from his hands.

What a way to spend a Saturday morning. He was still in bed when he got the call from his overnight supervisor about the malfunction, and since there was no one else around, Nathan drew the short end of the stick and had to come in.

Not that he was busy. He didn't want to be around anyone anyway. When he went to work yesterday, he barely spoke and didn't even go into his office. He headed straight to the machine rooms to keep his hands and his wolf busy; otherwise he'd go mad. After he clocked out, he went deep into the woods to shift and let his wolf run free. If he didn't, he'd surely do something stupid, like go the Blackstone Hotel and get on his knees to beg Violet to stay.

His inner wolf whimpered at the thought. *No way, buddy.* He wasn't going to let her sink her claws into his heart just so she could tear it to pieces again. Nathan was ready to give her the world, and she tossed it aside like it was trash.

His phone began to vibrate in his pocket, and he threw the rag aside then answered it. "What do you want?"

His sister's voice sounded annoyed through the receiver. "Where are you?"

"At work."

"Seriously? Well, drop whatever it is you're doing and come down to Rosie's."

"Rosie's? Why the fuck should I go there?"

"Just come. It's a matter of life and death."

He grunted. "Why do I gotta be at some baby shower? I thought you said it was girls only."

"Nathan Philip Caldwell." Kate was doing her best impression of Ma. "You come down here *now* or I'll tell everyone you wet the bed until you were thirteen!"

"I was twelve and it was one time," he protested. "And you were the one who put my hand in the bowl of cold water."

"Who gives a shit!" Kate exclaimed. "Just come down here now. Or else. I know your phone passcode and I can make your life miserable for all eternity."

"How the hell—Kate? Fuck!" He wanted to toss the phone against the wall. He knew who would be at the baby shower. *Goddamnit*. His wolf was scratching at his insides, urging him to go.

"Fine. Fine!" He would go and find out what Kate wanted, but he would avoid Violet at all costs.

———

Nathan was ready to do battle when he arrived at Rosie's, but he was clearly unprepared. Six very angry-looking women surrounded him as soon as he walked into the door.

"You're such an asshole!" Kate shouted.

Penny's face was red. "How could you—"

Catherine rolled her eyes. "I can't believe—"

Christina put her hands on her hips. "You have to—"

Amelia pointed a finger at him. "Make it right and—"

Steam was coming out of Sybil's nose. "You go and—"

The chaos of voices was too much, and he put his hand up. "Ladies, stop!" he shouted. "I'm not dumb, okay. I know who you're talking about."

"Did you really walk away from her?" Kate asked, poking her finger at his chest.

Is that what Violet told them? "Did she tell you *she* was the one leaving in the first place?" he shot back. "That I asked her to move in with me, and she tells me she hardly knows me after everything that happened?" He couldn't mask the hurt in his voice and he didn't care. They were only siding with Violet because she was a girl.

"First of all, you're an idiot," Kate said. "You didn't ask her, did you? You told her she was moving in with you like she had no choice in the matter."

"She's my mate. Was my mate," he corrected. "Her place is with me."

"But you couldn't ask her?" Sybil asked.

"I was making a grand gesture! I thought girls liked that shit."

"But you should have asked her," Penny said. "Gone to her properly and asked."

Oh shit. He realized they were right. He had been so excited at the thought he and Violet would have a home together that he didn't think she would even say no.

Kate glowered at him. "Second of all, do you know *why* she was leaving?"

He shrugged. "She was too good for Blackstone, I guess."

"She wanted to go back to Eritana to save those girls," Sybil said.

"She already saved them," he pointed out.

Sybil's eyes blazed. "Yes, but they're still in danger."

As Sybil began to explain what had happened, Nathan felt that pit in his stomach grow until it was the size of the Grand Canyon. She was going back for the girls? They were going to lose their home? He remembered what she said, about them being her cubs. Of course she would go back to protect them. She never even met Joanne, and she risked her life to save her. Violet was the most unselfish person he'd ever met.

"I didn't know," he whispered, his throat suddenly feeling dry. A sense of dread began to grow in him.

"We know," Kate said, placing a hand on his arm. "If it's any consolation, we think she should have told you. Nathan, you act like an asshole most of the time, but I know you would do the right thing."

"Then why bring me here for the sixth degree?" he asked.

"Because it was fun, duh!" Kate guffawed. "Now, are you going to go after your girl and tell her how you feel? 'Cuz I'm one hundred and ten percent sure she feels the same way."

"She does?" He wanted to believe Kate.

"There's only one way to find out."

"Shit!" He reached into his pocket for his keys. "Did she say what flight she was on? Which airport?"

Kate raised her phone. "Already sent it your cell."

Nathan kissed his sister on the cheek. "You're a gem! I gotta go."

The girls all cheered and wished him well as he waved goodbye to them.

"Fuck, fuck, fuck." He had to catch her before she left. He wasn't sure what she would do, but he had to at least tell her how he felt. He loved her with his entire being and would follow her to the ends of the earth if she wanted.

Nathan made a mad dash to his Mustang, not even bothering to open the door. He slid in through the open window. "Let's go and get her." The engine purred to life as he turned his key in the ignition.

It would be a long drive to the airport, even if he floored it. Reaching for the button on the radio, he flipped it on. At that moment a song came on, that old one about the guy walking five hundred miles to fall at someone's door.

"Ugh." He hated sentimental bullshit songs like this. But before he could change the station, the lyrics began to sink into his head. "Shit yeah!" He would walk five thousand—no, five *million* miles to be with her. He turned up the volume and stepped on the gas harder.

By the time he pulled into Verona Mills Airport Boulevard, it was 4:30. She was probably at the gate. "Shit, shit!" He'd buy a ticket if he had to.

As traffic slowed down when he neared the airport, he slapped his hand on the wheel. "Motherfucker!" Two cars had a fender-bender right on the on-ramp.

His inner wolf roared in frustration. "Don't worry. We'll get to her, buddy." He unclipped his seatbelt and opened the door, not caring if he left his car on the road.

Nathan ran the last three miles to the airport. It was 4:55 p.m. by the time he got to the ticket counter. "Give me any ticket you have, lady."

The girl behind the counter looked stunned. "Sir, where do you want to go?"

He slapped his credit card down in front of her. "*Anywhere.*"

"Er, yes sir!" It took her another five minutes to look on her computer and print out a piece of paper. "Here's your boarding pass. Enjoy your flight to Yemen!"

With a grateful nod, he grabbed the boarding pass and didn't bother to wait for his card. He scrambled toward security, cursing at the long lines. 5:10.

As soon as he cleared security, he sprinted toward Gate 101 for the 5:30 flight to London. *Almost there.* He pushed his body much harder than he'd ever had in his life, evading obstacles and people along the way.

"Stop!" he shouted as the gate attendants were closing the door. His heart slammed into his ribcage. "Don't close that gate!"

The two attendants turned their heads, their faces looking startled as Nathan skidded across the carpet and stopped inches from them.

The sound of the door closing echoed the doom he felt in his chest. "I need to get in there!"

"Sir, we've already closed the door."

"But—"

"Sir, FAA regulations state that—"

"I don't give a fuck about your regulations! I have to talk to her!"

"Sir, if you don't calm down, we're going to call security," the attendants said in a firm voice.

Nathan stood there, his body starting to go numb as the watched the plane pull away from the gate. This was it. She was gone. He felt like his entire world was crashing around him. His wolf howled in distress. "Violet. I need to tell her ..."

"Tell me what?"

He froze. Slowly, he turned around to the source of the voice. He must be hallucinating, because Violet was standing in front of him, her beautiful blue eyes wide with surprise.

"You missed your flight." He was so dumbstruck it was the only thing he could think to say.

"I didn't," she said. "I couldn't go."

"Why not?"

"I couldn't leave without telling you I love you."

"Violet ..." He put his hands on her waist and pulled her close. He pressed his lips to hers, tasting the sweetness of her mouth. "I love you too," he whispered.

She sucked in a deep breath. "You came all the way here to stop me from leaving?"

"No," he said with a smile. "I could never stop you from following your heart. Those girls need you. And you need them."

Violet stepped back from his embrace and gave him a dumbstruck look. "I don't understand."

"I wasn't going to stop you from leaving," he said. "I was going to ask you to wait for me. I'm going with you, Violet. To Eritana. To anywhere you want go."

"Nathan ..." Her voice trembled as she said his name. Taking a step forward, she pressed her body to his and wrapped her arms around his neck to pull him down for a kiss.

As their lips touched, he felt a warmth washing over him like a gentle wave. His heart clenched, and it was like something was wrapping around it, something soft and comforting like a down blanket yet it felt like it could be strong as steel. When he pulled away, he realized what it was.

The mating bond.

"You're mine now," he said. "Mate." His wolf happily agreed.

"Oh!" She put her hand to her chest. The contented purrs were strong and vibrant. "I can't believe … it's incredible." She laid her head on his chest. "I've never felt like this."

"Me neither," he said. "I never want to be away from you."

"What what about your job? Your family?" She looked up at him, a little wrinkle appearing between her brows. "You can't just leave everything behind."

"Don't worry about that. I'm not. It'll work out, Baby," he said, kissing her frown away. "I'm not leaving everything behind. I'm following *my* everything."

EPILOGUE

A FEW WEEKS LATER...

Nathan wiped the sweat from his brow as he stood back and inspected his work. *Not bad*, he thought. He grew up knowing how to work on cars and other machines, but he'd never built an actual structure with a roof and walls before. One of the construction workers working on the building, a middle-aged man named Gregor, gave him a thumbs up. He grinned back and returned the gesture.

This particular building was going to be the start of the second home in the orphanage compound so that they could take in even more girls.

A few days after their reunion at the airport, Nathan handed in his notice to Lennox Corp. His friends were sad to see him go, but they all understood and told him he would always have a place in Blackstone and with the company. Nathan and Violet hadn't discussed any long-term plans yet, but they both knew Antonia and the girls needed their help. Nathan packed his bags, reluctantly handed the keys of his Mustang to Kate, and he and Violet flew to Eritana.

It seemed they had gotten there just in time as the villagers had gathered as a mob to throw Antonia and her girls out of their home. Needless to say, they didn't just see the fury of the Golden Demon, but its wolf mate as well.

They scrambled to find a new home for the girls, but in the end it worked out. Nathan, with the help of funds from his friends, purchased an old abandoned mansion just outside Aldari, the capital of Eritana. They first renovated the house so the girls could have a place to live, and then they started making plans to further expand the property and the Black-stone Girl's Orphanage.

"Nathan! Nathan!"

He turned around and saw a group of the youngest girls crowded around him. "Hey girls," he greeted.

"Nathan, please!" the smallest one, Eva, said. "Do it, please?"

Tiny voices saying "Yes!" and "Please!" rang around him.

He rolled his eyes in fake exasperation. "Well ... all right. But you promise to keep studying your letters, okay?"

"Yes!"

He turned around, facing away from them, and then whipped his head back. Wolf ears popped from his head and he grew his snout, whiskers and all. Fur sprouted all over his face. This sent all the girls into a fit of giggles.

"Are you bothering Nathan again, girls?" Violet asked as she walked up behind them.

"Sorry, Miss Violet," Eva said. "We just wanted to see the puppy."

"Puppy?" Nathan asked in an incredulous voice.

"The Silver Puppy!" another girl screamed, and the rest of the girls joined her in chorus.

"Hold on." Nathan walked over to Violet, a sea of girls parting as they let him through. "You're the Golden Demon and I'm the Silver Puppy?"

"Probably something lost in translation," she said, a smile tugging at her lips and a glint in her eye. "Besides, they think you're cute. Like a pet."

He turned to the girls. "Puppy, eh? I'll show you puppy! Raaawwr!" He raised his hands and formed his fingers into claws. They giggled and screamed, running away from him as he chased them around the compound. He continued to run after them until Antonia called them inside for lunch.

"Whew," Nathan said as he sat down beside Violet. She had taken shelter from the hot sun under a large fir tree. "Those girls are giving me a run for my money."

"You hardly broke a sweat, love," she said. "Besides you've been working a lot."

"*You've* been working a lot," he countered, then reached over to cuddle her to his side. His hand snaked around over her belly. "I don't want you getting too tired and stressing our cub."

It was a complete surprise when they found out Violet was pregnant. She had felt tired all the time, and she was throwing up in the mornings. Even her tiger seemed extra stressed, like it was fatigued but restless. They thought it was just the heat or the stress from travel and renovations, but a week ago they both heard it. Soft but strong, it was the heartbeat of their cub in her womb. The chemical that had brought on her heat had probably obliterated her birth control too. Needless to say, they were thrilled.

"What did your parents say?" Violet asked.

"They said they'll be here next week," Nathan answered. They had both agreed to keep the pregnancy between them for now but wanted to tell their families in person. "They're still on that retirement trip with their friends, but they want to swing by to meet you. And yours?"

"They can come anytime, so let's see if we can hit two birds with one stone and have them over and make the announcement."

"You're so smart," he said, giving her a kiss on the nose. "Oh. I almost forgot to tell you," he fished his phone from his pocket, "Matthew said to check the account again. He and Catherine sent another round of funding when they heard the girls got into school for the next semester."

"Your friends are too generous," she said.

"They're not just friends," he reminded her. "They're *our* family." He scrolled through his mailbox, searching through the tons of new mail. "Weird." He frowned.

"What is it?"

"This must be a joke." He chuckled and showed her the email that read "Luke Lennox" on the "From" line. "I didn't even know Luke had an email address."

"Well? What does it say?"

"Let me check." As he read the single sentence in the email, his heartbeat began to speed up and his fingers tightened around the phone.

Violet gripped his arm. "What is it, love?"

"Blackstone. Everyone's in danger." He stood, dusting the dirt from his pants and helping her up. "I need to go." He looked around them. "We have enough people and guards here. You and Antonia and the girls will be safe until I come back."

Violet's eyes turned steely with determination. "I'm going

with you," she said. He opened his mouth to protest, but she placed a finger on his lips. "No. Like you said, they're *our* family. And when family needs your help, you go. Besides," she pulled him into a hug, "I'm following *my* everything. Wherever he wants go."

He smiled down at her. Even though he wanted Violet and his cub to stay here and be safe, he knew she'd fight him with every ounce of her strength until he relented. "All right. But this," he placed a hand over her stomach, "is our priority, okay?"

"Of course," she said. "Now, let's go save our family."

He couldn't love her more in that moment if he tried.

The End

Thanks for reading!
Want to read some bonus and extra scenes from this book, including some sexy scenes that are too hot to publish? Sign up for my newsletter here:
http://aliciamontgomeryauthor.com/mailing-list/

You'll get access to ALL the bonus materials from all my books, two FREE contemporary novels and my **FREE** novella **The Last Blackstone Dragon,** featuring the love story of Matthew's parents, Hank and Riva.

AUTHOR'S NOTES

WRITTEN ON MARCH 19, 2018

For authors, there are certain characters that are troublemakers. The ones who refuse to do what you want them to do or act how you tell them (I'm looking at you, Quinn). They keep you up nights or worry you, much like a child would worry a mom (Connor!)

I'm happy to say that Nathan was NOT like that at all. He was the baby who slept through the night (which meant I got some sleep), did as he was told and happy to play along.

Except maybe when it came to Violet.

I didn't know what to do with her. I wanted Nathan's interactions with her to be much different, but sometimes these characters have a life of their own. He refused to let her be weak, or even act as the "hero/rescuer". It was like, he was telling me that Violet was going to kick ass and be the hero in this story.

He even changed the ending. We've always read about heroes telling the heroines that they would follow them to the ends of the earth. And I'm glad that Nathan was the one to prove that saying right.

So now, we're almost at the end of Blackstone. Up next is Luke.

Oh my.

It's going to be a tough one. I suspect a lot of heartbreak for our hero. And for me too. Much like when I "ended" my other series (Meredith and Daric, Connor and Evie), I know I'll be a little sad to say goodbye.

Of course, if you know me by know, I'm pretty sneaky. I'll have more surprises for you!

Please feel free to email me at alicia@aliciamontgomeryauthor.com if you want to tell me what you think about my story.

If you really want to let your feelings known, leave me a review! It helps me out a lot as an indie reader.

Until next time!

All the best,

Alicia

PREVIEW: THE BLACKSTONE LION

This was not how Luke Lennox thought his day would go.

He certainly didn't expect to start it by confronting an entire biker gang, and then ending it with a suicide rescue mission with no backup.

Dr. Violet Robichaux didn't seem like it, but she could be one crazy chick. Barging into the old canning factory guarded by armed men only proved it.

"Fuck." He clenched his fists at his sides. "Let's go before she gets herself killed." He had barely finished his sentence before Nathan, Violet's mate, disappeared through the doorway.

Damn women, he muttered as he into the laboratory. Why was it even the most reasonable shifter males lost their fucking minds when it came to their mates. Even the notorious womanizer Nathan Caldwell was no different. *I don't even know why I give a fuck.*

Nathan's nose was probably sensitive enough to know

where Violet had gone to, so he followed the wolf shifter until they reached one of the rooms inside the factory.

"Don't you ever do that again," Nathan said through gritted teeth as he approached his mate.

"It's her," Violet gasped. "Joanne."

Luke came closer, glancing at the frail girl on the bed in the middle of the lab. This was the girl they had risked their lives for. His inner lion raged, seeing her state—dressed in a white paper gown, wires sticking out, her face pale.

Just when he thought humankind's cruelty had reached its lowest, they go and do something like this. *Those fucking assholes.* He looked around the room. It was as sterile as the rest of the facility, with various types of medical equipment all around. There were several beds, but only two were occupied—Joanne and another girl. As they had suspected, the factory had been turned into some kind of laboratory that experimented on shifters.

"Is she okay?" Violet asked as Nathan was checked on the other girl.

"Heartbeat's faint, but she seems to be hanging in there."

There was no time to lose. Gently, Luke picked up the Joanne. The scent of feathers tickled his nose. *Flight shifter.* Glancing over at Nathan, he saw he that he was lifting the other girl off the table.

Luke nodded to the door. "Let's get them out of here."

Violet's face was serene as she nodded in agreement, but he knew the animal she kept in reign was roaring to get out. Just like his lion.

The sooner they were out of here, the better. He'd never admit it out loud, but this place gave him the creeps.

They were only one step out of the lab when the alarms when off. Luke knew things would only get harder from here.

Nathan cursed. "Shit! They know we're here."

"Had to happen eventually." Luke nodded toward the exit. "C'mon. We need to get out in case they have lockdown procedures."

"Someone's down there." Violet pointed down the opposite end of the hallway. "She needs our help."

"We'll come back for her! Let's go now and save these two," Nathan insisted.

Thank God someone around here was thinking straight.

"No! I'm not leaving anyone behind!" Violet began to walk away from them.

"Goddamnit!" Nathan turned to Luke, and handed him the girl in his arms. "Get them out of here!"

Luke easily slung the second girl over his right shoulder as he tucked Joanna under his left arm. He gave Nathan an affirmative grunt as he pivoted and headed toward the door. Behind him, he could hear the pounding of boots and the sounds of clothes ripping as Violet and Nathan shifted into their animals.

Damn fools. They already had two girls. Why the hell were they risking their lives to save one more? The equation didn't make sense, but he didn't have time to think about it now.

Luke made it to the exit without incident, which solidified his earlier suspicions. This place wasn't well-protected. Its best defense was keeping a low profile. The factory had been abandoned for decades and no one passed by the old highway anymore. Which is probably why those bastards used it to conduct their experiments.

Thinking about what they could have done to these girls or any other shifter made his blood rage in his veins. But, there would be time for that later. Right now, he had to get these girls to safety.

Luke walked around to the front. It was empty, though there was garage. When he entered the rickety structure, he saw the nondescript Honda sedan inside.

Jackpot. It was even unlocked and the keys were in the ignition. These people really didn't expect to be discovered.

Luke placed the two girls in the back seat and shut the door. As he was about to get into the driver's side when he stopped, his hand frozen at the latch.

There it was again. The sound of a woman's voice. He heard it earlier, before Violet lost her shit and re-enacted her solo version of D-Day on the place. He initially ignored the way it made the hairs on his arms stand on end. But now, he just *couldn't.*

His lion roared, urging him to go back.

"We gotta go," he said in a gruff voice. But the animal ignored him. Damn lion had loved a fight. It helped feed the blood thirst that always seemed to be bubbling on the surface.

"Fine." He let go of the car door and strode outside, marching back toward the facility with purposeful strides. As he went inside, he saw two more guards running down the hallway, toward the door where Nathan and Violet had headed earlier. *Fuck.* As he shucked his jeans down, he let out a whistle, catching the guards' attention.

The two goons turned on their heels. They were so surprised at the fully-grown lion jumping toward them, they didn't even have time to raise their guns. He pounced on them, knocking one back so he slammed against the wall, while the other ended up underneath him. The lion let out a roar, before swiping a paw that slashed down the man's face.

"No!"

The sound of her voice was tugging at something deep in

his chest. The lion took over, and charged toward the sound, sprinting as fast as he could to the door at the end.

"You stupid whore!" someone shouted

As Luke sailed through the door, he saw a tall, man in green scrubs as he staggered forward. The small figure in his arms broke free, but the man's arms swung wildly. Luke saw something glinting in his hand that made adrenaline pound through his veins faster. Instinct told him he couldn't let that man harm her.

He bore down on the man, using his claws to scratch down his back, eliciting a screamed. Luke had never seen him before, but in his gut he knew this man was responsible for the suffering of many shifters. He didn't even think twice as he opened his mouth and sank his teeth into his head.

When the man stopped moving and struggling, he released the lifeless skull from his jaws. The lion stepped back, and began to change and shift.

As he transformed back into his human self, Luke grabbed a rag from a table and wiped off the blood from his mouth and chest. It would be a long time before he'd feel clean again, but it was worth it, knowing that evil bastard was dead. Was he the leader of this shadowy group that was hell-bent on killing every shifter in the world?

Luke threw the rag aside and glanced at the bloody mess on the floor. Someone as important as the head of an underground operation like this probably wouldn't have been this vulnerable or easy to kill. His instincts were telling him that there was someone higher up the chain.

The distinct clang of claws hitting metal caught his attention. Glancing to the side, he saw Nathan standing by a stack of cages. The scent of various furs, feathers, and scales hung in the air and Luke realized what those cages were for.

I'm going to tear all of them apart, then hunt down the bastards that did this. He strode toward Nathan, who had unlocked the cage with his claws. The other cages seemed to be empty, but—

Luke felt like he hit an invisible brick wall. As his eyes landed on the woman next to Nathan, his heart stopped, only to speed up at an alarming rate.

Mine! His lion roared.

He was so stunned, he hardly noticed the small figure that clung to her.

"Mommy," the little blond boy said in a hoarse voice. "The bad man ... is he gone?"

"He won't hurt you anymore."

The growl escaped his lips before her could stop it. It must have been loud enough, because it startled Nathan.

"Luke, you okay, man?"

Mine!

His lion's unearthly voice was the only thing he could hear aside from the roaring of his blood in his ears. Every muscle in his body tensed up. *It couldn't be. She couldn't be—*It took every ounce of his strength, but he managed to tear his gaze away from her and turn around.

"Luke! Where are you going?"

A muscle spasmed in his jaw. "Outside."

"Outside?"

"Yeah." There was a thickness coating his throat that he didn't even realize was there. Clearing it, he simply said, "Jason and Christina'll be here any minute," before walking away.

His lion fought him with each step that took him farther away from her. *We can't*, he told his inner animal. *We're not meant for a mate. This isn't right.*

His words were answered by angry growls.

"No!" he roared. *We can't have her. Besides, she's already got a man.*

Ugly jealousy reared its head, but he pushed it down. He didn't have the chance to look at her for long, but her image was burned into his mind. Plump, pink lips. Long brown hair like a mahogany waterfall. Large, soft brown eyes. A softly-rounded face. She was obviously distraught, but he could imagine her with a big smile that would reach those doe-eyes. Looking up with a sweet expression, not at him, but her husband, the father of her bear cub.

She could never be his. There had to be some mistake. He knew his lion was fucked up, so it probably got its wires crossed.

"Luke!"

He spied the familiar Range Rover parked next to the garage. Jason and Christina had finally arrived.

"What happened?" the dragon shifter asked.

"It's a long story but," he nodded at the factory, "Nathan and Dr. Robichaux are still in there. They're going to need your help."

"We're on it," Jason said. "Where are you going?"

"We found more kidnap victims," he explained. "I got them safe, but I should bring them to the hospital."

"Good idea." Jason clapped him on the shoulder. "You okay, man?"

"Yeah. Why?"

Jason shrugged. "I dunno. You just look a little … disturbed."

Luke's huffed. "If you went in there, you'd know why."

"Are Nathan and Violet okay?" Christina asked.

"They should be out soon." Without further explanation,

he marched toward the garage, to the girls he left behind in the car.

The breathing of the two women sounded normal enough, so he knew they'd be okay until they reached Blackstone Hospital's ER. Verona Mills was closer, but they'd be much better off in Blackstone than at some human-run place.

Forget about her, he thought as he turned the key in the ignition. He gripped the wheel tight and gnashed his teeth. She and her cub are safe, and soon, they'll be on their way home. That was all that mattered.

Made in the USA
Las Vegas, NV
27 November 2023

81685493R00121